MARIE-HÉLÈNE LEBEAULT
AUTHOR OF THE EVERS SERIES

THE QUEST
— FOR THE —
KRAKEN'S INK

DEFENDERS OF THE REALM - BOOK FOUR

BEACHES AND TRAILS
PUBLISHING

ABOUT THE AUTHOR

Marie-Helene Lebeault lives in Quebec, Canada and is the mother of two young adults. A retired teacher, she now spends her days writing, translating academic manuals, and lending her voice to corporate training videos. She enjoys reading, hiking, and going to the beach. She is also an avid rollercoaster fiend and is on a mission to visit all the Six Flags amusement parks with her daughter. Every year, she travels for three weeks on a solo adventure to a new part of the world.

Follow on Social Media, she'd love to hear from you!

www.mhlebeault.com

facebook.com/mhlebeaultauthor

x.com/mhlebeault

instagram.com/mhlebeault

amazon.com/author/mhlebeaultbookbub.com/authors/marie-helene-lebeault

bookbub.com/authors/marie-helene-lebeault

goodreads.com/mhlebeault

linkedin.com/in/mhlebeault

tiktok.com/@mhlebeaultauthor

youtube.com/@mhlebeault

ALSO BY MARIE-HÉLÈNE LEBEAULT

The Blood Mage

Blood Magick

Blood Legacy

Standalones

Clarity Castle

What Happens Next?

Ghost Stories

Holiday Shifters

Echoes of Tomorrow

Utopia

Picture Books

Fairy Grandmother: Millie Goes to Antarctica

Fairy Grandmother: Millie Goes to the North Pole

Fairy Grandmother: Millie Goes to China

Fairy Grandmother: Millie Goes to Africa

(Also available in French, Spanish, German, and Italian)

CHAPTER
ONE

THE AIR TASTED DISTINCTLY of salt. Wickham clutched at the stabilizing bar on the saddle slung over Herja's back. In her dragon form, there wasn't much he could hang onto. Though he and the other fourth-year witch students had learned to ride their dragon counterparts without saddles, he was grateful to have one on the five-day journey it had taken to get here.

Now, he admired the steel-grey tones of Nolen's massive dragon, the glittering turquoise of Penelope's form, and the various hues on the others. He had to admit; he found the sweeping colors of his mate, Herja, the most attractive.

From where he was, he could only see the emerald green of her back, with the occasional hint of amethyst along her sides. With her belly being royal blue, her color looked just like the Northern Lights. She was unique in every sense of the word.

Although, Wickham thought, *every witch thought that about their dragon*. Kaia gushed over the steely grey of Nolen every chance she got.

Their two professors for the year, Ealdwulf and West, angled downwards. Ealdwulf was a mud-brown dragon, sleek and lithe, while

West's brown clothes made him blend in with his mate's scales, if not for the silver beacon of his hair.

The entire group followed, landing lightly in a small area just above a slope leading to the beach. Wickham shook his head as he dismounted from Herja's dragon form.

Professors Ealdwulf and West were only twenty-seven each, and at seventeen, Wickham didn't feel much difference. It would be difficult to think of the two professors as 'adults,' let alone 'professors.' The fourth-years were the first group they'd be teaching on their own, although they had shadowed the two previous fourth-year professors for two years now.

Ten years seemed like a lot... and yet not much at all.

Herja shifted to her natural form and slid her hand into his as the students gathered around the professors. A thrill washed through Wickham, and he grinned. Holding hands might not be much for many people, but it certainly felt like leaps and bounds for his and Herja's relationship.

"Now that we're here, take some time to familiarize yourselves with the layout of the terrain. We choose a new spot for the camp every year, so you'll have to find the natural formations of the land that will serve you to build with," Professor Ealdwulf said.

Professor West nodded, pushing his silver hair behind his ear. "Remember the four most important aspects of a long-term camp. Shelter, food, water, and hygiene."

Herja raised her hand, then dropped it again. While most of their professors had insisted on raising hands before speaking, Ealdwulf and West had informed the students that, since this wasn't a structured classroom, they didn't need a structured talking system.

"Do you have suggestions on where to start?" Herja asked. "Is there a freshwater source nearby?"

West shook his head, a slight smile on his lips. "You know the rules. We're here to teach you lessons, helping you to learn how to communicate with one another over long distances and teaching you how to pace your magic. But the rest of it is up to you."

Herja frowned. "You're also here to advise us and ensure we don't die."

The other students laughed, some in genuine humor, others nervously.

Given the events of the past four years, starting with the old king of Odentia sending his brother, Finnegan, to kidnap them all from the Silver Springs when they first became dragons and witches, the professors at the Institute had given the fourth-year students the choice of changing up the traditions of this year.

Usually, it was just the students and their professors for the school year, with no contact with the outside world. It helped them learn how to deal with extreme circumstances and adapt to unseen events.

These students were pros at that—they'd dealt with unseen events every year so far!

The two Headmasters, Valiant and Twila, offered to allow the students to bring anyone they wanted. Ultimately, the students voted on it and went with the standard approach.

Tensions with Odentia had drastically decreased since the old king died and his daughter took the throne. And since they had dealt with worse situations in the past, they were looking forward to the banality of figuring out shelter and food rather than fighting off warriors trying to kidnap them.

"We are not here to figure things out for you," Ealdwulf said with a half-smile. "You'll have to do that yourselves."

Wickham nodded. That was one thing he was most looking forward to. This was a year where they would learn how to navigate their social interactions on their own. It was an adventure, as though they were the survivors of a shipwreck...

With a magic mirror that would transport them back to the Institute if things got too bad.

Herja turned to the other students. "I propose that the first thing we do is figure out some sort of leadership. That way, when things need to get done, we'll have a clear sign of who oversees what, so it doesn't get forgotten."

"I agree," Adina said, nodding. "We should list our major needs and have one person in charge of each section, understanding that we are all expected to help them in that area."

The others nodded as well. Wickham puffed out his chest, grinning. Of course, Herja would be the one to suggest their first order of business.

Herja pulled her famed bookbag from the pack that Wickham wore and reached inside to pull out a notebook and pen.

"Food, water, shelter, and hygiene," she said, scribbling them down. "Now, do we have any volunteers?"

"Wait," Kaia said.

Herja turned to her.

"Don't you think we should first set up a voting booth? I don't think we'll get into anything very controversial, but I think we should keep to the anonymous system," Kaia explained, running her fingers through her short silver curls.

"That's a good point," Xena said as he nodded, his glowing silver eyes moving to his mate, Jalene. "Don't you think so?"

"I agree," Jalene said.

The only human in the group, Victor, nodded as well. A glance around showed everyone had agreed. Herja tucked her book into her pocket.

Raven, their newest classmate, cleared their throat. "We could put a cup over on that log there, have everyone check their vote, and drop it in. If we want it truly anonymous, we'll have to have a ballot with all the names on it, so we can just check it off, and our handwriting won't give us away."

Wickham couldn't help but notice the tension in his classmates and even the professors when Raven spoke. It wasn't entirely unexpected. Even though Raven had integrated into their ear, several things kept a distance between Raven and the rest of the class.

For starters, Raven was a gorgon... at least, that's what everyone thought they were. If a creature looked into their face, it would be turned into stone. Raven also reported that their hair had become a nest of snakes. Very 'gorgon' indeed, and gorgons were the stuff of olden myths.

Second, Raven was a year older than them. Wickham didn't think this made so much of a difference, but since all the other students had gone through their school year together, it made sense that adding someone else in would be tricky to integrate.

This was especially true since the other students would never see what Raven looked like. They kept their face veiled at all times.

All in all, Raven represented a new form of magic that nobody was certain of. And even though Wickham had spent a great deal of time last year with his core group of friends, fighting Finnegan to rescue Raven, even he had to admit that he was nervous around them.

He wasn't happy about it, but he couldn't just change his feelings with the snap of his fingers, as much as he wished he could.

"Good idea," Penelope exclaimed.

She looked around sternly as though she was getting ready to defend Raven—this was one thing that surprised Wickham the most.

He expected Herja to be protective of them since she and Raven had been at the same orphanage for many years, but Pen had jumped in like a bodyguard, ready to throw hands with anyone with Raven. And Penelope wasn't the sort of person who turned to violence first thing... or ever.

"I think it's great," Wickham said as well, nodding.

It was important that they all got along. Once winter hit, they would rely on one another for survival. It wouldn't be impossible to get outside help, but it would not be easy.

"What do you mean by 'hygiene,' though?" Icarus asked Herja. "Won't it be easier if we just use the ocean as our toilet?"

Herja opened her mouth, but Victor cleared his throat. He was a young recruit in the military, but as he and Lena were mates, he was joining them this school year.

"You've used pit toilets, right?" he asked Icarus.

Icarus nodded.

"Think about how quickly they fill up. Now do you want that in the same place where we will have to go for food? The ocean is a great resource, but if we contaminate it with our waste, we risk driving out potential food sources away and making us sick," Victor explained.

"Not to mention, once winter hits, we'll be risking thin ice," Herja pointed out.

Icarus nodded again, looking satisfied with that answer. "So, hygiene is figuring out where to put the toilet?"

"As well as camp cleanliness," Herja said. "Dishes, options for bathing, all that sort of thing."

"What have previous years done?" Raven asked West.

Even though Raven wasn't a witch, their magic was more similar to that of a witch than a dragon, so they had been grouped among the other witches. The Headmasters of the Institute, along with the two kings and two queens of the Crown, had tried to give Raven a relatively normal experience.

"Last year, each person dug their toilet to last them over the year," West replied. "The year before that, they had buckets of sand that they emptied into a new hole at the end of every week."

Wickham wrinkled his nose. He didn't like the idea of either of those, although he supposed that if he had his own pit toilet, he would prefer to occasionally cover up the nasty smells with sand.

"I think maybe we should separate camp cleanliness from general hygiene," Kaia said. "Cleanliness falls more under daily chores. So that's something to add to it. Someone to coordinate daily chores. Cooking, cleaning up after cooking, keeping things neat, and all that."

Nods answered her. Wickham grinned. That was so easy to take care of.

They didn't take long to set up their 'voting booth,' along with volunteers for each major task. Each person stated why they thought they would be good at the job, and then the group voted.

There. Now they all had their major leadership roles to take care of, and the next thing was to decide the highest priority to complete.

A warm breeze came in from the ocean, distracting Wickham briefly. The water glistened as it lapped against the white beach. His grin spread wider. This was a beautiful place. He had a feeling that this would be their easiest school year yet.

CHAPTER
TWO

HERJA WIPED the sticky sweat from the back of her neck. Though winter was upon them, it sure was hot out.

"Hold up," Vera called from behind.

Herja stopped and looked back, seeing that her hunting companions—Vera, Jalene, and Icarus—had fallen back some distance. She grimaced as she adjusted the bow she had carved, now hanging on her back. She had been practicing all summer to prepare to build hunting weapons but wasn't entirely happy with what she had.

Of course, their primary hunting strategy would be trapping. It took less energy overall, and getting smaller game would be more sustainable than hunting large animals anyway.

The others caught up with her, and she took a moment to ensure they all had water left before continuing the trail. "If anybody needs to take a break, let me know," she said.

It was a little awkward for her to lead this hunting expedition. As much as she didn't think the big hunting trips would be efficient, they had already had difficulties with a big boar in their camp, rooting at their supplies and causing a mess.

Herja would have preferred this hunting trip only be dragons, so they could shift and defend against the boar if they came across it, but

Icarus was experienced in hunting, and Jalene was raised on a pig farm, and so knew how to dress the animal once they got it.

An intact male boar like this would not be pleasant to eat, but it would give them meat and protein. With the proper processing, an animal that size would last them well into winter.

Herja still preferred to be in charge of a different part of the camp. Penelope had been voted leader to establish their shelters, Adina was in charge of fresh water, Xena was in charge of sanitation, and Kaia was in charge of daily tasks. Herja was in charge of building their food stores. Which meant more gathering than hunting, something that the fourth-year class was already pretty good at.

Even though they had only been on the beach for a few days now, things were going well so far. They had enough supplies that they brought with them to last until the end of the month. With any luck, they could soon build up their stores so they wouldn't have to worry about food over the winter.

"I still think we should have been allowed to start at the end of last semester, so we could have the summer to grow food," Vera whispered.

Herja twisted her head, thinking Vera had become a mind-reader, but she was looking at Jalene.

"Yeah, that would have been good. But I guess this is part of the challenge, right? Depending on what circumstances we find ourselves in the future, we might not have access to crops," Jalene replied, though she sounded doubtful. She shook her head. "Yeah. I think this is one of those things that's outdated."

"But the challenge is kind of fun, don't you think?" Icarus asked.

Herja stopped walking, as the others had already. Clearly, even if they had said nothing, it was time to take a break. "I think it's more about teaching us cooperation in strained circumstances rather than survival skills," she said as she sat on a low log.

The others were quick to sit down, too.

Jalene cocked her head. "What do you mean?"

"Well... think about it this way. Until now, we've always had the adults there to solve our problems if something came up. Now, it's just the twelve of us with two hands-off professors. Tensions are bound to arise."

"I suppose," Jalene said, her brows pinched together.

"And this will teach us how to communicate with each other and solve our problems so that as we graduate and people come to us with their problems, we can better understand how to be mediators," Herja explained.

Icarus stretched his long legs out in front of him, a thoughtful look on his face. "You know, that makes sense. Although I'm not sure this is the best way to do it. I guess it's a mix, huh? I mean, I'd hate it if this year was changed. It's the one I've been looking forward to most."

"Me, too," Vera sighed, a dreamy look in her eyes. "I can't wait to meet the mermaids!"

"Oh, same," Jalene said.

Herja nodded. She was looking forward to that as well. At the end of the year, they would negotiate with the mermaids, a powerful under-water people with kingdoms and territories under the crushing depths of the sea just like they had kingdoms on land, for the final ingredient the witches needed for their spell books: kraken ink.

"I hope we get to see the krakens, too," she said. "I've heard they're magnificent."

"Yeah. I heard that sometimes you could find friendly ones that catch fish and other food for you," Jalene said excitedly. "I'm more excited about them than dolphins."

Icarus shuddered. "Dolphins are creepy."

Herja closed her eyes as she leaned against the tree, letting herself tune out the discussion of mermaids, krakens, and dolphins.

Now that she thought of it, it was odd that there wasn't much mention of mermaids during all the myths and legends she knew about the first people who eventually became dragons, witches, and humans. They were only in the myths of legend, which also held creatures like cyclops, qilin, pixies... and gorgons.

Other sentient beings like the Chameleon sprites were likewise not spoken of often, but mermaids were half-human... or at least, appeared to be it. So, were they descended from the first ones as well? Like how the sun created dragons and the moon created witches, did the sea create mermaids?

They had to have their own origin myths. Herja was desperately curious to find out what they were and if anything in their mythos could help Raven.

"You look pensive, Herja," Icarus said, breaking into her thoughts. "Is everything okay?"

Herja opened her eyes again. "Oh, I was just wondering if the mermaids came from a magical spring as well or if they have some sort of ceremony that gives them their tails. I heard their cities are built in giant air pockets, and they walk on two legs within them. But maybe the ceremony gives them their legs, and they're born with the tail."

"Huh. I never thought about that before," Icarus said. He turned his crudely made spear in his hand. It was good as a walking stick and to catch fish, but not to hunt a boar.

Of course, they weren't hunting it down for a confrontation. They planned to dig a pit they could use to drive the animal into, making it easier for them to kill.

Or maybe I should just take my dragon's form and snap its neck, Herja thought.

It made her stomach churn. As much as she knew it was vital for them to understand and process their own food, she wasn't looking forward to the killing part.

"We should get going again," Jalene said, getting to her feet. "Pigs are faster than you'd give them credit for, so if we're going to find its trail, we'll have to be fast about it."

Icarus stood as well.

Herja nodded. They didn't want to set a trap at camp for it, fearing that the mess and noise caused by its death would draw in big predators. She rolled her shoulders, then sighed. The sun was high overhead, and their hours of searching the forest hadn't turned up anything useful.

"We should call it a day," she said aloud as she batted at a fly. "I don't think this plan is working. We have found nothing that looks like it's directly from the boar, so we're in the wrong spot. We'll return to camp, grab the tools we need to dig and get ourselves a pit trap on a deer trail."

"Are you sure?" Vera asked. "It seems a waste to do all this searching for nothing."

Herja nodded. "It wasn't for nothing. We've got a better lay of the land, and we found those berry bushes, which need to be harvested right away before the animals eat them."

Icarus looked disappointed. "So, no more hunting and back to the grunt work, huh?"

"Sorry," Herja said with a shrug.

Icarus shrugged too. "Eh, I guess it's a learning opportunity."

That was a good way for all of them to look at it. Herja certainly needed the experience to admit that her first action plan wasn't working out. It did feel like a waste of time, even though they found other food sources.

But they'd get this boar. They couldn't afford to have it messing with their camp.

As they headed back to camp, Herja took the last place. Usually, she was impatient to move as quickly as possible, but she reminded herself of how Penelope would always take the last position when they were on hikes. She always made sure that the slowest person didn't get lost.

And during the summer, while she and Wickham watched over the thirteen-year-olds as they went to the Silver Springs, she had seen why that was so important when the group nearly lost a little girl.

Herja wasn't entirely sure she would pursue her political ideals anymore, but she was a leader here and now. She had to ensure she was acting like one.

"Oh, Herja," Vera said, twisting. "I heard that Professor Farrow is going to adopt you. Is that true?"

"Don't listen to rumors," Herja said flatly.

Vera winced and turned back to the front.

Herja bit her lip, feeling queasy. Was that too rude? Perhaps she should have politely told Vera that it was between her and Row and that she didn't want to talk about it.

Or maybe that was too much to share.

The truth was, Herja had mustered up all her courage to ask Row to adopt her. Last year, she had asked them for help in getting adopted. After spending most of the summer with Wickham, Row gave her several potential families' profiles.

She hadn't looked at any of them and mustered her courage to tell them the truth. She didn't want to find an adoptive family; she wanted them and their mate to adopt her.

Row said they needed to talk to their mate about it. Unfortunately, Herja had waited so long to actually tell Row about her desire for them to adopt her; she had gotten here before she had an answer.

Now, she wondered how much trouble she'd get in if she used the travel mirror to return to the Institute for answers. She felt like she couldn't breathe when she thought about waiting almost a year before knowing.

They trudged silently for a while, while Herja's thoughts got even more twisted. Her head ached, and she called for another rest.

"Next time we do one of these things, we need to bring food," she said, settling down on the forest floor. "I didn't expect to be out this long."

"I thought about food but didn't want the extra weight," Jalene admitted.

Herja frowned. "That's what my book bag is for, so we have lots of room to carry supplies without weighing us down."

Jalene shrugged. "Are you sure it's accurate to call it a book bag anymore? Cause it seems to me that—"

A sudden, sharp noise made them all jump. Herja turned just in time to see a huge brown-black shape barreling toward them—the boar.

Then it was on them, sharp tusks flying this way and that.

CHAPTER

THREE

KAIA SANG as she scrubbed clothes in a large pot of water. She didn't particularly enjoy washing clothes in the same vessel they cooked their food in, but until Adina and Xena figured out a way to build a bathing tub, it was the only thing they had where she could get hot water.

Otherwise, she'd be at the small spring Adina discovered, scrubbing dirt and grime off the clothes there.

"Kaia," Professor West called as he approached.

She waved happily, moving the shirt she was working on into the basket where the other clothes were.

"Where are the others?" West asked, looking around.

"Pen took everyone up the ridge to bring down wood for digging. She figures that the most important step is to dig ourselves a cellar that we can use to store food in because getting food will only grow more difficult, but we can always build above the ground, even when there's snow." Kaia watched the professor's face, hoping for a sign of what he thought about it.

West had a superb poker face, though, and only nodded. "And so, you're left cleaning up the camp by yourself?"

Kaia shrugged. "It needs to be done, and I prefer domestic labor over digging and chopping."

West sat across from her and wrung out the clothes. "Yeah, I under-stand that."

"Pen also wants to cut out some sod bocks or figure out how to bake clay into bricks to build ourselves an oven," Kaia added. She grinned, proud of her friend's ideas. "I think it's going to work out. Winter will be difficult but not impossible."

"And Ealdwulf went with them?" West asked.

Kaia nodded.

"I'd better go find them. I got a message from the nearby mermaid village that they're sending a representative to talk with the students soon," West said, standing again. "You know where they went?"

Kaia pointed. "Penelope was hoping to go half a kilometer that way."

She said it was best if they went farther to collect their supplies before winter hit, leaving the closer resources to collect once the weather turned.

West nodded and jogged that way. Kaia watched him go, then returned to her work. Long-distance communication was tricky and exhausting, from what she'd been told. It was generally reserved for emergencies.

So far, they hadn't started learning how to tap into that. She was eager to do so, however.

Kaia finished washing the clothes, then rinsed the soap from them and hung them up to dry. Soft footsteps sounded behind her as she put up the last pair of socks.

She turned to find a woman approaching her. Hair in fluffy curls that fell to her shoulder shimmered in shades of blue and green. She wore a simple brown shift dripping at the hem around her knees, and her skin was damp.

"Hello," the woman said, cocking her head as she peered at the clothesline behind Kaia. "What are you doing?"

"I'm just hanging up our clothes to dry," Kaia said. West had said the mermaids would arrive shortly. "Are you from the underwater village?"

The woman nodded. "I'm Lyra."

"Kaia. Pleased to meet you." Kaia held her hand toward the mermaid.

"The pleasure's all mine," Lyra said, taking her hand. Her grip felt like a limp fish, and she rubbed her fingertips against Kaia's knuckles unpleasantly.

Kaia broke the handshake as soon as she could without seeming rude. "So, you're our contact with the mermaids this year?"

"Indeed, I am. And you must be one of the new students from the Institute. I'm excited to see what you will offer us this year," Lyra said, looking around the camp. She headed toward where their packs were hanging from a tree and reached for Adina's. "What's in here?"

Kaia hurried over and intervened. "Personal belongings. Please don't mess with them."

Lyra lowered her hand. "But I need to see what to ask for in exchange for kraken ink."

"You will see what we offer when the time comes. But these are our belongings to get us through the winter. I must ask you to back away from them," Kaia said firmly, holding up a hand. She had heard that mermaids lack a sense of boundaries, but she hadn't expected to deal with it so dramatically.

Lyra wrinkled her nose. "Show me around your camp then, Kaia. Maybe we can trade for other things. My people are expert hunters; if you want to get food from us, you'll have to provide things we want."

Kaia bit her tongue. As beautiful as mermaids were and as alluring as they were portrayed in stories, she was already growing tired of Lyra. Maybe it would be better if others were here... she took a deep breath and smiled.

Maybe Lyra just needed some time to adjust to how humans did things.

"We really don't have much of a camp right now," Kaia said, gesturing around. "This is our firepit, and then we put out our things every night to sleep and pack them back up in the morning to avoid getting pests in our sleeping things. We plan on building a good-sized building right about here, though."

She moved to a level spot and gestured around herself.

Lyra joined her and wrinkled her nose. "This is going to be too small."

"Well, we know we'll need shelter to keep warm through the winter. And our priority is to get the minimum requirement done before the weather turns and build up more structures as necessary," Kaia explained.

She looked around the area. Yes, it would be cramped. But it was just big enough for the fourteen students and two professors to sleep, especially since they planned to build it tall enough to have a loft and hammocks that could be hung one above the other.

"Once we build our main house, we can start working on other ones," she continued. "Right now, we're planning on three other sleeping houses, then a bathhouse as well."

"A bathhouse," Lyra repeated. She fluffed her hair and shook her head. "I always find it so strange that land-goers have lived in dirt and then think they need to wash the dirt off them."

Kaia laughed at that description. "It's not exactly right. I mean, we have little choice. We have to live 'in the dirt,' as you say. Our bodies aren't exactly equipped with fins and gills."

Lyra laughed. "But you could just bathe in the ocean."

"It's going to be too cold for us soon, and besides that, the salt will dry us out."

"I see," Lyra murmured.

Judging by her expression, though, she really didn't. Kaia couldn't help but wonder if mermaids understood how their land-goer bodies weren't built to handle the salt of the ocean. While mermaids absorbed the liquid they needed and had special glands that expelled excess salt, it didn't work the same as if you were a witch or a human.

However, some dragons had that adaptation and were well-suited to ocean life.

"I like this thing," Lyra said, pointing at the pot near the fire. "I want it."

"Er—"

Kaia's confusion was interrupted but the sound of beating wings. She looked up in time to see Herja's dragon form swooping down, along with Vera's forest-green dragon. Both dragons landed in the cleared area where the house would be, with Icarus and Jalene clutching to their backs.

Kaia briefly looked at Lyra, who looked intrigued, then raced over to help. They were supposed to be out gathering food. Had something happened?

As she approached, the scent of blood hit Kaia's nostrils. Her heart jumped to her throat as Icarus and Jalene, both on Herja's back, slid down her smooth side to land on the ground. Jalene was supporting Icarus, and when Herja and Vera both shifted back to their natural forms, blood soaked through Vera's pant leg.

Kaia rushed to Vera and grabbed her around the waist, supporting her as she trembled. Vera's face was pale, but she still nodded her thanks to Kaia. They hobbled toward the firepit, where several logs were set up for the students to sit around it.

"Where's Wick and the professors?" Herja asked Kaia as Jalene helped Icarus down.

"They were collecting wood half a kilo that way," Kaia pointed. She pulled off her belt to tie it around Vera's leg, uncertain how bad it was. She looked up to Herja. "We're going to have to use mind-to-mind communication."

Herja stared in the general direction the others went, then took a deep breath. She knelt on the ground and closed her eyes.

Kaia trusted Herja had done her own research into long-distance communication, despite not having much time being taught yet, and turned her attention back to her injured classmates. Icarus's shirt was soaked through with blood, and he looked like he was having difficulty staying upright.

"Let's lay you both down," Kaia said. They'd only get more hurt if they fell over.

Jalene and Kaia helped Icarus lay down, and then Kaia retrieved one of the freshly washed shirts while Jalene helped Vera. Returning, Kaia folded the shirt, spread it over Icarus's abdomen, and put her hands over the injury.

Icarus let out a grunt, his face paling even more.

"I'm sorry," Kaia said miserably.

"Don't be." Icarus closed his mouth then like he was afraid of throwing up.

"The boar attacked us," Jalene explained. "It came out of nowhere, and then it was gone before we even knew what was happening."

Kaia's heart dropped. She'd seen that big, ugly animal with its enormous tusks. They were so dirty, even if the injuries weren't bad—the amount of blood spoke differently—the risk of infection ran high.

Herja opened her eyes, lifting her head. "I made contact, I think. Wick should know."

And she promptly keeled over.

Jalene left Vera and checked on Herja, only to announce that she seemed okay, just exhausted. The grumbles Herja let out seemed to back her up, so Kaia focused on Icarus. She used the wand Nolen had carved her to cast a couple of spells, helping her two injured classmates be more comfortable while also slowing down the blood flow. She didn't dare try to stop it entirely, not when she didn't know the extent that her spell would go.

Lyra seemed bored watching them and wandered over to the fireplace, where she tried to collect the fire, not the pot. Kaia ignored her as she kept her classmates talking, monitoring their color and overall well-being.

Soon enough, more dragons swooped over the forest and onto the high ground where they had camped. Wick jumped off Penelope's back and rushed over, his gaze sharp and focused.

"What happened?" he demanded, digging into his herb pouch. He caught sight of Herja and faltered.

"She's not injured, just exhausted from contacting you," Kaia said quickly. "Come here—Icarus has an abdominal injury, and Vera injured her leg. I've been keeping pressure on Icarus's injury, and we did a tourniquet for Vera's leg."

The two professors joined them, and Ealdwulf knelt beside Icarus next to Wickham.

"Let me see," Ealdwulf ordered.

Kaia lifted her hands and the bloodied shirt. They inspected

Icarus's stomach while West looked at Vera's leg. Kaia hurried over to the fire and grabbed the soap, scrubbing the pot quickly before filling it with fresh water and putting it over the coals to boil.

As she added wood to the fire, Lyra suddenly gasped.

Kaia's head lifted. Lyra's pretty face was twisted in hatred and fear as she pointed at Raven, who stood close to Penelope.

"Why have you brought a diseased demon to my ocean?" Lyra demanded.

CHAPTER
FOUR

PENELOPE'S HACKLES rose as she planted herself in front of Raven. Diseased? Demon? She glared at the green-haired person standing near Kaia and the fire.

"Who are you?" Penelope demanded. "Never mind, I don't even care. Never talk about Raven that way again. They are part of the Institute here, and if you ever talk about them that way again—"

Raven took hold of Penelope's arm. "Stop."

Penelope continued to glare at the intruder, even though she was well aware of the shocked stares she was getting from everyone around her. Part of her wanted to drive this person off, but she also knew this was a knee-jerk reaction caused by worry, stress, and physical tiredness.

Well, that and she was still working with Raven to stop them from thinking of themselves as a monster. Raven had been going to therapy, but out here, there wasn't exactly a therapist's office they could skip to. Penelope still thought they should have had a counselor of some sort brought along, but Raven kept insisting that it would be weird.

"Who are you to talk to me like that?" the interloper said, drawing into a puffed-up ball. "If we were in my village, I would have you publicly reprimanded!"

"Okay, let's not get too worked up," Kaia offered, sliding to stand between Penelope and Lyra. "Pen, this is Lyra. She's a mermaid and the representative we'll negotiate with at the year's end. Lyra, this is Penelope. She's... well, basically our leader. Has been from the start."

Not that Penelope had asked to be their leader... but she had to admit that she had indeed taken on that role over time. Hers was the only vote that everyone agreed on.

Lyra narrowed her eyes at Penelope. "And the... other one?"

Penelope tensed again, but at least Lyra hadn't outright insulted Raven this time.

"Raven. They're a good friend of ours and one of our classmates," Kaia said. "And since they are friend and classmate, please don't refer to them negatively."

Penelope didn't like how... polite Kaia was in the face of such utter rudeness. She kept her mouth shut, though, continuing to glare at Lyra. If the mermaid were their contact with the negotiations at the end of the year, they would need her.

"I can't promise you that," Lyra said, turning to Kaia. "Her presence offends all mermaids—"

"They," Kaia, Penelope, and Herja all said simultaneously.

Although she looked utterly exhausted, Herja had pulled herself to sit on a log. "Raven is non-binary, and you will respect their pronouns if you expect any negotiations with us in the future."

Odele, Xena, and Adina were working at various spots on the camp, responding to the orders Wickham and the professors gave them as they took care of Icarus and Vera. Neither seemed to be on death's door, which Penelope was grateful for. She wasn't sure she had the attention to care for everything happening.

Lyra folded her arms over her chest and nodded. "I apologize for misgendering you... *Raven*. Even if you are a gorgon."

Raven let out a shaky breath. "You can tell without even seeing me?"

"I can taste the magic you carry," Lyra replied.

Kaia's eyes lit up. She turned more fully to Lyra again. "We know little about gorgons anymore—maybe you can help us learn more? If Raven could control her magic more—"

"I will *not* help a gorgon," Lyra snapped.

Penelope leaned forward, a growl in her throat, but Raven tugged on her arm. "Let's just go. Let Kaia deal with this."

Penelope wasn't sure she wanted to do that—but it suddenly occurred to her that Raven wouldn't want to hear this. After everything they'd been through, the last thing they needed was to be forced to stand here, listening to some random mermaid call them diseased and a demon.

"We'll be working when she is gone," Penelope called over her shoulder as she spun on her heel.

She headed toward the site she'd picked for the root cellar. Close enough to see what was going on but far enough that the discussion wouldn't reach them.

Once there, Penelope grabbed one of the few shovels they'd brought and dug at the hard ground.

Raven collected a second shovel and thrust it into the ground. "I wish you wouldn't get so angry."

Penelope flinched. She had never thought of herself as someone who was easily angered. But this last summer, she'd been finding it challenging to keep a lid on her temper. "I'm sorry. I don't know what's going on with me. I thought I was supposed to be finished with puberty now."

Raven laughed softly. "I don't think that it ends that easily. But I think we both know why you're so angry."

"I don't," Penelope said.

"So, you're going to say that you're not angry that the Headmasters of the Institute weren't able to restore me to my human self?" Raven asked bluntly.

Penelope winced. It wasn't exactly like that. But she didn't like that Raven's entire existence was such a source of debate. "I just don't like the way people treat you."

"Most people aren't like Lyra."

"Lyra is, though, and you heard Kaia. She's supposed to be our contact for the negotiations?" Penelope tossed her shovelful of packed earth onto the pile just outside the boundaries she had drawn for the cellar. "I don't like it."

Raven was quiet.

Shortly after, Kaia joined them, telling them that Lyra had returned to the ocean. "Pen, I know you were just defending Raven, and I can't blame you for it—"

"Then why does it sound like you're going to?" Penelope glared at Kaia.

"I was shocked, too," Kaia said, lifting both hands in defense. "I never would have expected Lyra to respond that way. She wouldn't say anything about gorgons, though, and I can't blame you for defending Raven. I just think it's best if you have little to do with the mermaids."

"Me or Raven?" Penelope demanded, putting her hands on her hips.

Kaia ran a hand through her hair. "Both, I'm afraid. I'm sorry, but we can't afford to offend the mermaids. They're our only hope to get the kraken ink, and without that, none of us witches will complete our spell books."

Penelope opened her mouth, then closed it again. She couldn't blame Kaia for worrying about the possibility of getting that vital resource from the mermaids, not just for their year but all the witches that would come after them, too.

"I don't mind having nothing to do with the mermaids," Raven said, their tone even and clipped. "I'd rather not be called a 'diseased demon' again."

Penelope drew in a deep breath, forcing herself to calm down again. That was a good point. She didn't want to deal with the mermaids, anyway, so why was she so ready to fight Kaia on this?

"I'll be taking charge of the mermaid interactions for now," Kaia said, rubbing the back of her neck. "Lyra seemed to be interested in how we exist, and since I'm going to be the person who sticks close to camp most, it makes sense."

It did make sense. Penelope thought they probably should have another vote on the matter, but she was too tired to care. The tension of her anger disappeared, her body felt overheated, and she felt a deep regret at how quickly that anger had built.

Even if she had been defending her fated mate at that moment, she didn't want to be the sort of person who got angry and flew off the handle.

Penelope swallowed, her throat feeling sticky. "Thank you, Kaia. And I'm sorry for snapping at you."

Kaia smiled at her. "I know. It's okay. Do you need a hug?"

"A hug would be wonderful," Penelope said gratefully.

She stepped forward and hugged Kaia. It was a relief to know that her friend was so easygoing and would easily forgive her mistake. It wasn't Kaia's fault that Lyra had reacted that way to Raven, and now Kaia had figured out a solution to the problem...

At least a temporary solution.

Penelope pushed that thought aside. It would work out.

She, Kaia, and Raven returned to the others. Instantly, Lena and Victor were bombarding Penelope with questions.

"Should we keep digging the root cellar or build the house?"

"Should we have a separate quarantine building for Wickham to treat people's injuries?"

"What are we going to do about the mermaids?"

"How are we going to get that boar to make sure this doesn't happen again?"

Penelope held up her hands, causing the others to fall silent. A weight settled on her shoulders, even though she tried to ignore it. "What happened, exactly?"

Herja pulled herself to her feet, still pale but steadier now. "We were attacked by the boar that's been hanging around. Wick and the profs say Vera and Icarus aren't in life-threatening condition; their injuries were shallow considering the situation, but they'll need to stay on bed rest for a few days, maybe a few weeks."

Penelope nodded her thanks to Herja.

"I figure I'll take the other dragons, and we'll hunt down that boar," Herja said. "Using our dragon forms if necessary. You and the witches will be better suited to building the house. I know you wanted to dig the cellar first, but we can use a house to store the food to start with. Since we've got injured people, they need a clean, protected space to stay in."

Again, Penelope nodded. That made sense.

"And what about me?" Victor asked, a frown creasing on his face.

Penelope turned to him. "Would you be good to keep digging with Raven? We're getting close to the clay; once we can make bricks, we can build ourselves a good kiln and smokehouse and all that."

Victor hummed, glancing at Raven.

Tension crept back into Penelope's neck. If he was going to protest working with Raven—

"I think that will be fine," Victor said. "Are you up for digging, though? I thought you were saying you were having shoulder troubles this morning."

Raven's face veil fluttered at the edges as they shook their head. "I'm fine. I might need extra breaks, but I'm good to work."

Penelope breathed out, rolling her shoulders to relieve the lingering negative emotions. She felt like anything could set her off again, and that wasn't a great place to be. How could she stop herself from feeling this way, though? She wasn't sure.

"Is everyone all right with this?" Herja asked, looking around at everyone.

Nods answered her.

"Right. Then let's take an hour and eat, drink, try to cool off, and then we'll get going again," Herja said. Her shoulders were rigid like she expected someone to argue with her.

Nobody did. Instead, everyone slowly dispersed to get at their own things. Herja took a deep breath, then approached Penelope and Raven. Worry shone in her silver eyes.

"You both okay?" she asked under her breath.

"Yeah, I think so," Penelope said.

Raven nodded, then said, "I'm fine. Hungry, though. I'm going to set up my blankets so I can take off this veil."

They gestured at their face, and Penelope opened her mouth to say she'd help, but Raven had already turned away.

Had Lyra's words hit Raven closer to home than they would admit? It wasn't as though Penelope could read them well, not when their face was covered like that. If she could see their eyes, that would be one thing...

But she thought Raven wanted to be left alone. So, Penelope sat down, pulling out her waterskin to drink. *Just breathe,* she reminded herself.

They had a long, long year to go.

CHAPTER
FIVE

AFTER LYRA'S INITIAL VISIT, Kaia didn't see her for two days. That day, she showed up when everyone else was gone and wandered around watching Kaia work for almost an hour, demanding Kaia tell her stories. It was entertaining enough to have company while everyone else was working or resting in Vera and Icarus's cases.

The group had put together a temporary log cabin, smaller than the initial plans but good enough to meet their immediate needs. Three days later, Lyra hadn't come back to camp.

It was probably because Raven's shoulder had been preventing them from doing any of the heavy work with the others, so they remained at camp to help Kaia.

"I'm just happy that we're finally going to have a bathtub," Kaia said as she and Raven sat on either side of the large wooden crate that Herja had built the previous night.

Raven was slathering the outside with mud, and Kaia was going after them, putting spells on the mud to turn it into stone.

Kaia had considered asking Raven if they'd be comfortable turning it into stone themselves but ultimately decided not to. Raven couldn't control their abilities, and Kaia didn't want to make them more uncomfortable in their own body than they already were.

"Me, too," Raven sighed. "We'll have to seal the inside, too, so it's still much work to be done. Although I think on the inside, we should try to temper the wood and use natural means to seal it, rather than magic."

"Oh, agreed. Don't want to get into the middle of winter and have the tub fall apart because the spells wore off," Kaia said in an upbeat tone. She enjoyed spending time with Raven, but the reminder of how unintentionally deadly Raven could be made her heart skip a beat. "Er... how do we do that?"

"First, we're going to need a good oil to rub down the wood with; get it nice and soaked in so that will give it some natural waterproofing," Raven said, then paused. "Well, another thing we can do is to soak it in water, making the wood swell, and then since we have it cast in this stone, there isn't anywhere for the wood to go, so it'll press together. Like a wine barrel. Then the oil for an extra coat of protection."

Kaia nodded. "You know a lot about these sorts of things."

"My parents work at hot springs. I pick things up." Raven sighed as they worked again. "It's nice to help."

"But you did help your parents before," Kaia protested.

"All I could do was sit around darning socks. As much as I hate what that second spring turned me into, I am glad it cured my illness."

Kaia pointed her wand at the last bit of mud, turned it to stone, and stowed it away. "Hey, if I'm overstepping, please tell me I am... but I think we should talk more about that whole 'actually help' thing you said."

Raven's head twisted toward her, but Kaia couldn't tell if Raven was annoyed or curious without seeing their face. "Why?"

Their tone was guarded. Kaia swallowed, choosing her words carefully. "Okay, it's like this. You said that you didn't help, then said that you darned socks. I know you did a lot of sewing and craftwork. That's all extremely important labor."

Raven was quiet.

"I know it's easy to forget," Kaia pressed on, hoping her words were hitting where she wanted them to, "But especially since you were working with hot springs, that is vital. Bedspreads, doilies... that's what makes people comfortable."

"I'm pretty sure they come for the hot springs, not the doilies," Raven said dryly.

"So... Do you think it's useless labor that you were providing clothing and beautiful things?" Kaia asked directly. "Wickham's mother is a seamstress. Are you saying she doesn't do 'real' work?"

Raven shook their head. "No. That's not what I'm saying. I just... I'm happy to be more physically able."

Kaia stood and stretched. "See, that's what I thought you might be actually saying. I just wanted to show you that words matter... I know it's hard, but sometimes it helps to change what we say to be more positive."

"That's what my therapist says. She also said I'm allowed to mourn the life I thought I'd have."

"I'm overstepping, aren't I?" Kaia asked, wincing.

Raven hummed, then said, "A bit, yeah."

"Sorry."

"You're coming from a good place. I appreciate that."

Kaia nodded once. "Can I ask you something else? Related but not entirely?"

Raven sighed. "Yes."

"Well, I've been working on crocheting mine and Nolen's star threads into a blanket. Nolen made a bunch of flax fiber that we've spun into a lovely yarn with our star threads, but I'm getting perplexed with the pattern. So, I was wondering if you know how to crochet and if you did, if you'd help me out."

"Oh. Um, sure. I can try," Raven said, sounding cautiously optimistic.

Kaia smiled. "Great! I'll get the pattern, and you can look through it while I fill up this bad boy with ocean water. I don't want you to strain that shoulder more."

"I can help," Raven said, their voice dropping now.

"Yeah. After you look at the pattern, I'll have you start a new fire and cook supper. It's too early yet, and there's nothing else to do," Kaia explained. It occurred to her that Raven would be especially sensitive to being 'shunted to pity work' as her aunt would say.

Kaia didn't like that phrase, but she would try to be sensitive to avoid making Raven feel like they were being placated.

They started back to the main cabin when suddenly distant shrieks and screams filled the air. Kaia turned to Raven, and Raven's head turned toward her. Without a word, they rushed down the hillside toward the ocean beach.

There, they found mermaids dragging themselves from the water and racing nude up the beach, screaming, faces blanched with terror.

And behind them, in the roiling sea, massive tentacles rose and reached for the fleeing figures.

<hr />

HERJA'S LUNGS ached by the time she got to the beach. She wasn't even sure what instinct had triggered her to return to camp, but with the rest of the dragons taking flight, they must have sensed the same thing.

They arrived to chaos. Mermaids dodged this way and that as they raced up the hill from camp to the ocean while massive krakens dragged themselves ashore, their tentacles lashing out.

Herja caught sight of a head of silver curls amid the chaos—Kaia!

She dropped, blasting out a fireball at the kraken on the shore. There were at least three more trying to climb out after it. The flames hit on rubbery red flesh, and a piercing shriek made Herja's ears hurt. She flew down, dropping between the kraken and Kaia, while the other dragons followed suit.

She spread her wings wide to prevent the krakens from reaching the fleeing mermaids and let loose. Beside her, Nolen's steel grey form had never been more welcome as a continuous stream of fire ate up the space between them and the krakens.

The deep-sea creatures retreated before the flames, still screeching out that horrible noise until they disappeared again beneath the waves.

Herja trembled as she took her natural form, the light blue uniform they had all gotten at the beginning of the previous year magically adjusting itself once again.

"What happened?" Xena asked, sounding stunned.

Penelope turned toward camp. "Let's go find out."

She led them up the hill to where the witches had brought the mermaids. By the time the dragons reached them, all the mermaids had been given some sort of covering. Herja narrowed her eyes when she saw Lyra was wearing one of her shirts, but she ignored it.

Better than having to see these mermaids running around buck-naked.

"Thank the sea you were here!" Lyra sobbed as she clung to Kaia. "I don't know what would have become of us if you weren't. I have never been so frightened in my life—I thought we were going to die!"

Penelope fell back and tapped Herja's hand. Herja stopped, leaning in closer to Penelope.

"I can't talk to them. Every time I see Lyra's face, I want to punch it," Penelope murmured. "I need you to take the lead here."

Herja nodded her understanding. After the way Lyra had verbally attacked Raven, she wanted little to do with the mermaid, either. But she was used to masking her emotions and could do what she needed to do in this case.

Although maybe since this was extraordinary circumstances, the professors would want to take charge? Herja glanced at them, but they were whispering to each other some distance away.

She shook her head. "Lyra. Tell us what happened."

Lyra lifted her head. Her eyes and nose were dramatically red, just as it would be on any land-goer. Her lip trembled. "It was just a normal day. We were going about our lives when suddenly, those krakens attacked. They destroyed the village shields, ruined our houses, and ripped apart our crops. We barely survived."

Herja glanced at the mermaids. There were about two dozen of them. "Your village only had this many people?"

"Yes. It's temporary, just until the surface freezes over and we head back to the city," Lyra replied.

Several others nodded.

Herja pushed her ink-black hair from her eyes. "Why did the krakens attack? They're supposed to be docile."

"We know that," Lyra said, her snarky attitude reappearing. She let out a heavy sigh. "I don't know why they attacked, all right? They just did, and we were nearly killed. We can't go back, not with the krakens in the water. We'll have to stay with you until the danger is passed."

Oh, no. They had got the boar, which meant they had a good supply of meat, but it wouldn't last long with another twenty-four people. They were falling behind what Herja wanted for stored food at this point.

But with the mermaids, they'd at least be able to increase the amount gathered. Herja dragged a hand through her hair, looking at the ocean again. The krakens still surged just below the surface. It wasn't like they could just send the mermaids back to the sea, not when the krakens were waiting to attack them again.

"We'll have to make it work," Herja said. "In the meantime, you can all rest, and we'll figure out what we need to do. Hopefully, you'll only have to stay for a few days."

At this, Lyra nodded. "Agreed. We wouldn't want to stay with—"

Her eyes darted toward Raven. Penelope was standing near them, and she tensed. With her red hair catching the sunlight and her muscular arms flexing over her chest, she looked incredibly intimidating.

"Stay with?" Penelope pressed.

"With you land-goers, when we are unaccustomed to living on the land," Lyra replied quickly. Her green-blue curls blew into her face as she turned back to Herja. "But we will, of course, be extremely grateful for your aid."

Herja didn't like that the decision was all on her—but she nodded. "Kaia, can you make sure that we have enough clothes for them all? We'll talk later. For now, though, let's figure out what we'll do for supper tonight."

Nods answered her. By all rights, they should have a vote about this decision... but again, Herja didn't think it would make much of a difference. After all, they weren't the sort of people who tossed others into danger.

"Pen, Raven, why don't you both come with me, and we can check the traplines?" Herja said quickly. For one thing, it would be good to get Raven away from the glares being sent at them.

For another thing, Herja needed Penelope's backup on this one. They were going to have to come up with a game plan for dealing with this unexpected upset.

CHAPTER
SIX

TWO DAYS LATER, the krakens were still hanging out in the ocean; the mermaids were still taking up all the room in the students, hastily made houses, and frost was on the ground.

Penelope pinched a rigid, frozen blade of grass between her fingers, watching as the delicate white lacing around its edges disappeared. The rest of the camp was still sleeping in their bedrolls around the fireplace, except the two professors who were currently hauling water from the springs to fill the bathtub.

Not that they used it as a bathtub right now. With so many more people in their camp, they went through the tub daily, using it as drinking water.

Penelope quietly built up the fire, noting that a few of her classmates did that peek-through-the-lashes thing that people did when they were awake but didn't want to be yet. She reached over to flip Kaia's blanket over her face, showing that she needed to sleep more.

After Kaia had stayed up half the night dealing with Lyra and the mermaids, she deserved the rest.

At least they knew the mermaids would sleep until noon.

And they were all mer*maids*. The female 'maids' lived in their own kingdoms, and the male 'tritons' had theirs. Fortunately, despite this apparent strict binary, all the mermaids respected Raven's non-binary status. This was a good thing because if the mermaids didn't extend such basic courtesy, Penelope might lose it.

She shook her head as the fire flickered back up, warming the area. Raven didn't talk about how they felt about the situation, leaving Penelope feeling off-balance.

Odele slipped out of her bedroll and yawned, then came to the fire. "What's the plan today?"

"We'll get working on the other cabins," Penelope replied. "I figure we can build one big house and divide it into rooms afterward easier than a bunch of smaller buildings. With the amount of frost and the increased population, we need to make sure everyone has room to have a roof over their heads."

Odele nodded as she settled down next to the fire. "Herja was talking about going on another hunt, hopefully catching a few elk we can smoke and preserve. For being underwater beings, the mermaids certainly eat a lot of meat."

And very little of the other foraged foods. Penelope sighed heavily. "Can you keep an eye on the fire? I need to go talk with the professors."

Odele nodded again.

Penelope grabbed one of the empty buckets and trotted toward the spring, a hundred yards away. It occurred to her that they'd need to build something over it, too, so they could trap the heat of a fire and prevent the spring from melting.

She reached the spring just as the two professors filled their buckets again. They both greeted her with a nod, and Penelope set her own bucket down.

"We need help," she said.

The two glanced at each other and pulled their now-full buckets to the side of the springs. Ealdwulf nodded at her. "Please continue."

Penelope dragged a hand over her fire-red hair. She'd been brushing and braiding it every morning and every night before sleeping, but it was getting greasy and knotted all the same. "We need help!"

"Help in what way?" Ealdwulf asked.

Penelope bit her tongue at the sarcastic response she wanted to say.

Instead, she took a deep breath to calm herself. "We need you two just to take over. Okay? We're not equipped to handle this."

West ruffled his shaggy hair. "Why do you say you're not equipped?"

"We have a bunch of mermaids among us, and they're not doing anything but demanding Kaia entertain them all the time. Every time anyone asks one of them to do anything, they claim they don't know how. So what are we supposed to do?" Penelope demanded, putting her hands on her hips.

"Does everyone feel this way?" West asked. "We can 'take over,' as you say, but it needs to be something that at least most of your class-mates agree on."

Penelope shrugged, frustrated. "I don't know. I haven't talked to them about it. If it weren't for the mermaids, we'd be fine. Well, maybe not fine, but this is more than we signed up for."

Ealdwulf nodded. "Then you need to call a meeting and—"

"Why should I be the one to call the meeting?" Penelope snapped, throwing her hands into the air. "Everyone's always asking me what to do, but I'm supposed to be in charge of housing! Not *everything*!"

West answered. "Penelope, I can see this is stressing you out. That's the reason to call a meeting. Because you have things you need to talk about and set boundaries with everyone."

Penelope glared at him. He didn't understand. She shouldn't have to set boundaries; she shouldn't be the only one so hyper-aware of all the moving parts of their group.

"If it were Kaia here saying that we needed to take responsibility for the mermaids, we would tell her the same thing, to call a meeting," Ealdwulf told her gently. He hesitated, then said, "And it's okay to step down from leading the housing, too. If you are overwhelmed, there is no shame in saying you don't want to lead anything."

"Why can't you just take responsibility for the situation? Deal with the mermaids, and let us deal with ourselves?" Penelope groaned. Even asking for a meeting to tell everyone this felt too heavy a burden.

Ealdwulf spread his hands. "Because you as students haven't come together to tell us to. Until it's a group request, we won't intervene in the way you choose to handle it all."

Oh. That actually made sense.

"Herja has been stepping up for a lot of your communication, too," West reminded her. "If you don't want to call a meeting, you can ask her or your friends to do it for you."

Penelope wasn't happy with that answer, but she understood where the professors were coming from. When she stepped back out of her feelings to look at the situation, she could see that she needed to discuss the case with the other students.

If she didn't like them coming to ask her questions outside of her scope of housing, why should she think she had any right to make this decision for them?

Quiet with her thoughts, she filled her bucket and carried it back to camp. While the professors resumed their work, Penelope sought Herja. By this time, the other dragon was awake, in their cellar, and double-checking their inventory.

"Herja. We need to talk," Penelope said.

Herja tensed. "What did I do?"

Penelope blinked, startled. "Nothing. I meant, we need to talk about the situation."

Herja let out a sigh and nodded at her.

"We need to have a group meeting to decide whether we're going to keep trying to handle the situation by ourselves or—"

"Why isn't breakfast ready?" a voice interrupted behind them.

Penelope stiffened as she turned. Sure enough, Lyra stood with a pout as she peered past Herja and Penelope into the cellar. How much of their conversation had she heard or seen the two of them and interrupted?

"We're having a private conversation," Penelope told her coolly. "Breakfast will be at the same time as the last two days. If you're hungry, you can help Kaia and the others set camp so we can start cooking sooner."

Lyra folded her arms. "But I don't understand all these land chores."

"Great, but you do understand what 'Herja and I are talking privately' means, don't you?" Penelope snarked.

Lyra narrowed her eyes, then flounced herself back to the others.

Herja sighed as the mermaid left. "You didn't sleep again last night, did you?"

"Is it that obvious?" Penelope flinched. "Something about her just sets my teeth on edge."

"I know. You haven't been acting like yourself lately."

"That's what I need to talk about. We need to have a meeting to decide whether we're going to keep on like this or if we're going to ask the professors to intervene, at least as far as the mermaids are concerned."

Herja sucked on her teeth as she nodded. "Yeah, we do. Lyra claims she's a princess, you know. And I'm not sure that she's lying."

Penelope flinched again. If Lyra was a princess, they were even further beyond their wheelhouse than she thought they were. "We can't keep going like this."

"Winter is coming," Herja agreed as she looked at the sky. She put a hand on Penelope's shoulder and nodded once. "Let's get back to the others and see if we can discuss this. With any luck, the profs will have something they can do about it."

The two of them headed back to the rest of the camp, where more and more mermaids were stumbling out of the cabin. Which was odd, considering they weren't usually up at this time of the day.

"Kaia," Penelope started as the witch headed toward them.

"No time to talk," Kaia huffed, rushing past. She hurried to the cellar and filled her wicker basket with food.

"I'll help her," Penelope said to Herja. "You go get things organized for the vote."

Herja nodded and headed toward camp while Penelope turned to help Kaia.

"What do you need me to help you with?" Penelope asked.

"We don't have any eggs," Kaia said, her tone stressed as she opened one chest they stored food in. "No eggs, no onions. I can't make an omelet."

Penelope frowned. "Omelet?"

"Lyra wants an omelet."

So much for not knowing about 'land food.' Penelope lifted her hands, stopping Kaia. "We're not feeding them individually. I know you're in charge of food, but taking orders is not sustainable. Just make the oatmeal mush we always have."

Kaia bounced on her toes. "Lyra said that—"

"Lyra has done nothing except order you around."

"She wants to take the mermaids hunting," Kaia snapped, her eyes narrowed. "And we could really use their help in that."

Penelope opened her mouth, then closed it again. Part of her wanted to push back against Kaia's choice of words. They didn't need the mermaids' *help*; the mermaids needed to contribute to their own upkeep.

But that was semantics and not worth arguing with Kaia about. Penelope saw the same stress she had woken up feeling in her eyes.

"And it's good for them to hunt, especially since we're getting low on meat," Penelope said. "But we can't cater to them. There's too many, and we have too much work around here."

"We have too much work? I don't see anyone else helping me when I'm cooking and cleaning and—" Kaia bit off her words, her eyes widening. "Oh. Oh, I'm sorry. I didn't mean to lash out at you. You've been working hard to get us prepared for the winter. I know that."

Penelope took a moment to calm her own reaction to Kaia's defensiveness. This was precisely what she was talking about—the mermaids didn't contribute and only made everything more difficult.

"Do you need someone to stay behind and help you today?" Penelope asked.

Kaia shook her head, though her expression said otherwise. "I can handle it. It's more important to get the buildings and food."

"If the mermaids are going to hunt, then we can all concentrate on building the next house," Penelope suggested. "Which means we will have people to spare to help you around camp."

"You don't understand. Lyra won't go hunting without her omelet. And we have nothing for an omelet."

"Maybe she will, once we explain the situation," Penelope said doubtfully.

She didn't. And with the mermaids already lounging in the camp, the students didn't hold their vote, either. So, Penelope brought Raven, Jalene, and Wickham with her to get more supplies for the day's work.

And nothing was resolved.

CHAPTER
SEVEN

WICKHAM FROWNED at the pink scar along Icarus's stomach where the boar had gored him. He didn't know exactly how long this sort of injury was meant to be rested. The tusks hadn't gone deep, not even cutting through the abdominal muscle, but it was still in a dangerous place.

Via magic, Wickham had closed up the injury and thought it would be okay for Icarus to get to work again. It looked like it was healed, but Wickham knew these things could be tricky.

"I think you're healed enough to help Kaia around camp," Wickham finally said. "As long as you don't haul water."

"Wickham, come on," Icarus let out an annoyed huff as he pulled his shirt back on. "It barely hurts anymore."

"And I don't want my spells to come undone and for you to rip it open again." Wickham rubbed his eyes and sighed. "It's only been a week, Icarus. So let's give it another week, okay? I would ideally have you in a proper hospital, but... yeah."

Icarus nodded, his stubborn expression softening. "I don't want to lose any more time in my education. Not after—"

He cut off, rubbing his chest, where a thick, rigid scar was hidden under his shirt. Wickham glanced away, knowing what Icarus meant.

He had ended up injured during their first year, being cut across the chest by Finnegan while defending Kaia. The injury had kept him out of school for a long time.

"Does it still hurt?" Wickham asked, nodding toward Icarus's hidden scar.

Icarus dropped his hand. "Not anymore. It's years old and has fully healed. So no reason for it to hurt."

Wickham sighed as he thought about those days. "When I think about what happened and how little I knew compared to now, I'm surprised I didn't accidentally kill you and Professor Lee during that time. Any of the magic I used trying to help could have left lasting damage."

"You kept us alive, though," Icarus pointed out. "It's useless to think about that time and wish you did things differently because it's over, and we're here now."

"Let me see your injury site again."

Icarus rolled his eyes but lifted his shirt. Wickham inspected the area, his brow furrowed. He really didn't have the training to know if the inside was healing like the outside. How long did these things take to heal?

When Tara was born, and Mother had to have a c-section, it took her six weeks to heal. This wasn't as intensive an injury as that, though, and Mother also hadn't had intensive healing spells put on her, either. They hadn't had a doctor in the area who was also a witch.

"Let me help Kaia around camp," Icarus urged, looking anxious. "The mermaids have been driving her crazy. And I'm going crazy, too. You let Vera get back to work."

Wickham narrowed his eyes at Icarus. "Yeah, I did. Because Vera's injury differed from yours, and it wasn't as bad."

Icarus groaned. "I need something to do besides listen to Lyra talk to herself!"

"All right, all right. Work around the camp pit is," Wickham agreed with a laugh. He had already said that, after all. And with how lazy the mermaids were being, Kaia really could use help.

Maybe, if they could get caught up on everything that needed to be done around here, they could start their lessons again. Ealdwulf and West were still teaching the students, but with the sheer amount of work that had to be done every day, more often than not, they were too exhausted to practice.

When they left the second log cabin, the one, the students would use from now on, they found Herja facing against Lyra. The mermaid sat on a log, arms wrapped around herself and tears dribbling down her cheeks.

"Then learn!" Herja bellowed, sounding more furious than Wickham had ever heard her.

Wickham hurried over, the constant tension of the situation coming down on him at once. "What's going on?" he demanded.

Herja pointed at Lyra. "She just ruined our nut stores by throwing them into the fire!"

"I was hungry," Lyra replied. "And I didn't know your land food gets ruined that way. You keep telling me to make my own food, and when I try, all you do is yell at me!"

Kaia stepped in front of Herja and Wickham. "I'll handle it, Herja. You, Wick, and Icarus go collect more nuts—er, I mean, if Icarus may go?"

Wickham hesitated, then shook his head. While it would be helpful to have Icarus with them to make it go faster, he wasn't comfortable with his patient running around all over the place.

"I'm supposed to help Kaia today," Icarus said. "Since she was in charge of daily chores but has done them all rather than just being in charge of them."

He exclaimed it, and Wickham winced. He'd been noticing the heavy weight put on Kaia, too. More than once, he thought about telling Penelope, Xena, or Herja not when they asked for his help, so he could stay and instead help Kaia.

But in the end, Kaia had assured him that it would pass. The krakens would move on any day, and the mermaids could return to their village...

Only the krakens continued to patrol to where the students

couldn't even go fishing, and if they went to the tide line to collect clams, one dragon had to be in their dragon form the entire time.

It wasn't Wickham that got the pointed look from Icarus, though; it was Lyra. And Lyra was too busy picking nut husks out of her—well, Kaia's—skirt to notice.

Herja shot one angrier look at the mermaid, then nodded. "Come on, Wick. And you," she said, pointing at Lyra, who looked annoyed, "stay out of the food stores. We can't afford to have you messing it up all the time."

Lyra flicked her hair. "Very well. Next time you ask for help—"

"Next time I ask for help will be the last time," Herja said, her voice flat. "We're getting fed up with you profiting off our labor and doing nothing to return it. So either you will contribute here, or you can find your own camp."

She stalked away, and Wickham hurried after her.

The truth was that he agreed with every word she said. But he also knew they couldn't just kick the mermaids out. Not when the witches would need ink at the end of the year.

Something had to give, in any case. The only question was, would it be the mermaids, or would the students finally crack?

⁂

"THAT IS A VERY, VERY RUDE CHILD," Lyra said, folding her arms.

Kaia ignored her, biting her tongue. While she was trying to remain polite and positive, the truth was that she was getting close to snapping. She couldn't afford to do that, though. She was the only one that Lyra sort-of listened to, and if she blew her top, Lyra would stop responding altogether.

"Icarus, can you clean up the lunch dishes and go through camp, making sure that there aren't any food scraps lying around?"

No matter how much she impressed on the mermaids that they couldn't waste food, every day, she found someplace where the mermaids had thrown away the bits of food they didn't like.

Today was the second day that Lyra had promised she and the mermaids would go hunting, but she had fought with Penelope this morning because Raven was 'bothering' her. Literally, all that happened was Lyra was playing with the fire when Raven went to refill her bowl with oatmeal.

This was becoming beyond intolerable. That Lyra acted like nothing was wrong was all fine and dandy for her. She would skip off to the ocean sooner or later and return to the city where she could have all the food the other mermaids had stored.

Lyra didn't realize how important it was for the students to have a store they could rely on. It had gotten to where Penelope wasn't even considering building more structures; she and the others spent every spare moment going out and collecting food.

And the cellar wasn't getting much fuller, either.

Icarus started the cleanup, and Kaia breathed deeply through her nose. One problem was that the mermaids were clearly bored.

Well, she had a plan to help fix that if she could get them to engage.

"Lyra," she said, turning to the mermaid, "I thought that, since you and the other mermaids don't know how to do much on land, today would be a good day that I teach you."

Lyra was playing with the fire again. She poked a long stick into it, spreading the coals closer to the fresh wood she'd put in. A suspicious look crossed the mermaid's face as she frowned.

"What do you mean?"

Kaia smiled, trying to appear extra friendly. "Today, we need to get laundry done, but there's so much I can't do it all by myself. I can show you and the others how we clean up our clothes and teach you a few songs to help."

Lyra dropped her stick and stood. "I don't think I want to. Your friend was rude to me."

"My friends are stressed, and you were in the wrong. I know you didn't know," Kaia continued, lifting a hand as Lyra opened her mouth. "But think about it. Wouldn't you be upset if someone came and wrecked something you were counting on?"

Kaia felt like she was talking to a toddler.

But Lyra's frown smoothed, and she nodded. "I guess so."

"Well, it will help everyone for you and the others to be able to help around the camp. It's boring to sit around doing nothing. Unless you wanted to go hunting?" Kaia suggested. *Please say yes. I want you out of here.*

Lyra waved a hand. "It's too late in the day for that now."

"Then you'll be fine helping me wash the clothes," Kaia said brightly. "I've already prepared the tub with some nice hot water and brought the clothes over. Everyone can come over and watch, then wash two or three articles themselves. It's going to be a lot of fun!"

Lyra grinned happily. "Oh, Kaia! I wish everyone were like you."

Despite her annoyance at Lyra and the mermaids, Kaia had to admit that it felt good to hear.

She led the mermaids to the tub and showed them how to scrub the clothes. It wasn't a great clean; they didn't have the supplies they needed, but a good soak and scrubbing against the tub wall was better than nothing.

All the while, she sang the song that she'd been taught by Madame Adora when they used to do house chores together.

Lyra watched while everyone else worked, and the tub was filthy when the clothes were clean. But the clothes were hanging up to dry, the biggest task taken off Kaia's list for the day.

"I don't think I enjoy living on land," Lyra said once the mermaids scattered and Kaia cleaned the tub. "I wish the krakens would go away so we could get back to my beloved sea."

"I'd like to know why they attacked at all," Kaia said off-hand.

Lyra grunted. "They probably know that we'll be getting their ink soon and don't want to—"

The mermaid cut herself off, eyes widening like she hadn't meant to say that.

Kaia straightened, shocked. "What do you mean? How do you get the ink?"

"That is not for land-goers to know," Lyra snapped, then flounced off, leaving Kaia to clean the tub and ponder her words.

CHAPTER
EIGHT

"DAY four of the mermaids claiming that they're going to go hunt and then calling it off," Herja groused as she pulled her hood over her damp hair.

The sky was a depressing grey with a constant misting rain falling. Not enough to prevent them from actually working, but enough to make it miserable. She was so exhausted by all this that she was about ready to go to the professors and demand to return home, regardless of the vote.

She wished she knew who the people who had voted to keep trudging forward were—no getting the professors to help them out, no turning any of the leadership roles over to them, no heading back home, not even contacting the Institute for backup.

What she wanted to know was why they would vote that way. Penelope resigned from her leadership position, citing a need to relieve her mental health. Somehow, the attention for everything shifted to be evenly split between Adina and Herja, then.

It was no wonder Pen was on the verge of a mental breakdown if she had to deal with this amount of pressure without asking for it.

"And there's a kraken," Raven sighed.

The two of them stood on a cliffside above the beach. Yesterday there had been no kraken sightings, but now they had proved again that they were still out there.

Herja groaned, rubbing her hands over her face. "I feel like we're in the middle of a powder keg. Sooner or later...."

Raven nodded, then turned from the sea. "At least we caught that deer and found those cattails."

"Yeah. At least we're getting somewhere in building our food stores." Herja gestured toward the creek where they had fish traps built. "Have you had any more dreams?"

Raven hummed as they stepped over a pile of dead underbrush. "Yes, but I can't understand them. I keep seeing visions of stormy seas and know something is happening, but it feels like we're still at a cross-roads. Nothing is clear the way it was on Thunder Ridge."

"I wonder if your prophetic abilities are linked to the springs, them," Herja said. "In the old stories, gorgons stayed in pretty well one spot. Maybe there are links to the magic there that weaken the further away you get?"

Raven didn't answer this, not that Herja expected them to. It was still a touchy subject, after all.

Herja just wished that Raven's prophetic powers were more straightforward. Something that they could flex and strengthen, become more adept at it, and trigger on command. Unfortunately, it didn't appear that was the case.

And, of course, the ancient stories were so frustratingly vague on the whole situation that it made them useless for the most part.

"I wish I could help more," Raven said once they reached the creek. "The mermaids are getting more agitated around me. Penelope was talking about leaving and doing our camp, but I don't trust them. My absence would only help if I went through the mirror."

"Do you want to go?" Herja asked.

"I don't want to give up," Raven replied, somewhat cagily.

Herja kicked off her shoes and rolled her trousers up to her knee before she waded into the ice-cold creek. She shivered, grinding her teeth. It wouldn't be long now before the creek froze over. Not that the fish traps had actually given them much bounty.

Today, like most days, it was empty.

"It's not giving up prioritizing your safety," Herja called over her shoulder. "I don't know if I'd stick around if...."

"If it weren't for Wickham?" Raven asked.

Herja nodded as she returned to the bank. Wickham wasn't going anywhere, not when he thought the class still needed him. Which technically, they didn't, as both Ealdwulf and West had medical training. But that was Wickham. He had to stay to make sure he could take care of everyone.

It was what she loved most about him. She would not risk that changing, not for a temporary situation. Worst-case scenario, the mermaids would stay with them over the winter. It sounded like torture, but the thing was, winter would only last for a few months.

And Lyra couldn't keep making excuses not to pull her weight around camp.

"There are other reasons why I'm staying, not just the 'give up' angle," Raven said once they were on the trail again. Their face veil slightly muffled their voice. Today, it was forest green with birds embroidered on it.

"No?" Herja asked.

Raven shook their head, climbing over a log and offering their hand to help Herja. "No. The mermaids know something. I've read the books of old legends, and there's nothing on gorgons other than the most superficial information. But Lyra recognized what I am without even having to see anything."

That was true.

"So you're hoping they'll tell us something that can help?" Herja asked.

"Exactly."

Herja hummed. She had also had that through, but trying to get the mermaids to divulge any information was like pulling teeth. They were so secretive.

But then, they had an entire culture that Herja knew nothing about. Maybe there was a good reason for them to be cagey.

They crested to the top of a hill just above the treeline. Herja reached out to stop Raven and gestured to the ocean behind them. "It's beautiful, isn't it?"

"It really is," Raven agreed.

The two students stood there in silence for some time. The trees closest to them were pines and cedars. But as the forest swept toward the ocean, it turned first to birches and oaks, then berry bushes, before fading into a rocky hillside that eventually became a sandy beach. The waves glistened white in the sunlight, contrasting with the dark shadows within it.

Even knowing the krakens were still there, Herja couldn't help but feel a sense of peace as she gazed at the ocean. It made her think of vitality, life, and adventure.

"Storm clouds are on the horizon," Raven murmured.

Herja searched the edge of the world, where the sky met the sea. She saw nothing but didn't doubt Raven. Storm clouds gathering... and what else?

✼

EVEN THOUGH SHE wasn't supposed to be the 'default leader' anymore, Penelope was often pulled into these situations anyway, especially when Herja wasn't around.

And that was how she was here, standing with her arms folded over her chest as she glared at the mess of food scattered from the cellar to the camp. Lyra and the mermaids were arguing with Kaia, and Penelope just bet that they were pleading ignorance again.

"I'm about ready to throw hands whenever I hear her whiny mouse voice," Adina growled beside Penelope.

Penelope nodded. This was getting tiresome. It was the second time now that the mermaids had raided the food storage and wasted several days' worth of the store. She was just glad that Herja and Raven were out collecting from the traps rather than being here. The last thing she wanted was for Raven to be caught in the middle of the mermaid's blame game.

Somehow, it was all Raven's fault that they weren't comfortable enough to go hunting to support themselves. Whatever that meant.

"There, I've finished my locks," Jalene said, stepping back.

Penelope had asked Adina, Lena, and Jalene all to put magical locks on the storehouse. She hated that it had come to this, but with the mermaids causing this trouble, they needed to ensure that only the students and professors could actually get at the food.

"Thank you," Penelope said to the three witches. "Hopefully, that will resolve that issue."

Lena sent a dark look to where Lyra was still arguing with Kaia. "And hopefully, it won't make additional issues arise."

"Ain't that the truth," Jalene grumbled. She jerked her head toward the camp. "Let's see if any of this stuff is salvageable."

Penelope stepped after them, but Adina took hold of her wrist. "Wait. I want to talk with you. How about we take the wheelbarrows and go collect some firewood?"

Staying busy did seem like a necessity. All the time. Even when they weren't busy, Penelope felt the pressure of needing to be busy... Was this what adulthood was like? If it was, she didn't want it.

It seemed that whatever Kaia had said to Lyra had gotten through to her since they weren't arguing anymore. All the mermaids had retreated into the first cabin, which they still claimed as theirs.

How did all twenty-four of them stay in there without crowding each other? Not that it mattered, Penelope supposed. She was just grateful that they left the second cabin to the students, although the two professors had built their own cabin to share at this point.

Another thing Penelope was actually kind of grateful for. It made the situation feel less like the professors were kicking around doing nothing and more like they were waiting for the students to make their own decisions and come to them for help when needed.

Once she and Adina had collected the wheelbarrows, Penelope led the way to the piles of logs they had cut down, ready to be chopped into smaller chunks and hauled back to camp.

"What did you need to talk about?" Penelope asked when they used the double-sided handsaw to transport the logs into chunks.

"I was wondering how you're holding up," Adina puffed.

Penelope looked up in shock. "What?"

Adina yanked on the saw, but Penelope's falter had gotten it stuck, so she gave up. "How are you holding up? I've noticed that even though you said you don't want to be in charge of anything, people still go to you when Herja and I aren't around."

An uneasy feeling twisted Penelope's stomach. "I'm doing as good as anyone else. Do you think it was my mistake to step back like I did?"

"Goodness, no!" Adina shook her head. "I'd be doing the same thing if I had as much pressure as you were put under. I'm sorry for my part in it, too. We assumed you would be our leader and stopped remembering that we have to lead ourselves."

"I feel responsible for fixing everything still," Penelope admitted.

Adina frowned. "Do we need to have another meeting? To remind everyone about the boundaries and to put more structure in place?"

"I don't think that will help."

Adina looked at the saw, her pretty face twisting into a scowl. "Yeah, I guess. We need to have a good long meeting about the mermaids and then be able to stand together and get them to actually listen and... you know, do what they're supposed to do."

"Instead of causing more and more trouble," Penelope agreed.

"Exactly. But even if we were all standing together and insisting on change, I'm not sure anything actually would change." Adina's expression grew even darker.

Penelope frowned. She was always caught up in taking care of the day-to-day things, and she avoided the mermaids based on their treatment of Raven. What was she missing?

"What do you mean?"

"Lyra keeps saying she can't help with this or that because she doesn't understand. She wrecks things, cries, and begs for forgiveness because she didn't know better."

Penelope leaned forward. "You think she's lying?"

Adina rubbed her eyes. "On the one hand, she reminds me of a toddler. On the other? A master manipulator. All I know is that something isn't right—and I think Lyra is pushing us to our breaking point for some reason. I just don't know why."

Raven.

Lyra was pushing because she knew the students wouldn't send them back to the sea while the krakens were there. But if the students became desperate enough for food? Lyra could easily leverage her dislike of Raven for the promise of a hunt.

"We have to get back to camp," Penelope said urgently.

Adina looked up in surprise.

"Leave the wheelbarrows—this can't wait," Penelope said, turning on her heel. She didn't listen to Adina's shout of protest as she raced back down the way they had come.

She had to get back to camp before the mermaids turned against her mate.

CHAPTER
NINE

PENELOPE ARRIVED at the camp to find Herja and Lyra standing nose-to-nose, screaming at each other. Her heart plummeted as Herja gestured at the large pile of wasted food now sitting in buckets to be disposed of.

"How are we supposed to feed ourselves if you keep ruining our supplies!?" Herja shouted.

"We're going to do a hunt! Why are you so controlling?" Lyra yelled back.

Penelope slowed as she got to them, drawing herself to her full height. She wanted to scream back at Lyra, but that wouldn't do any good—not if Adina was right about her manipulating them, which seemed far too likely for Penelope to take the risk.

Instead, she physically pushed herself between the two. Herja fell back a step, grunting, while Lyra lifted her chin and met Penelope's eye.

"Control your people, dragon, before they cause problems," Lyra snapped.

Penelope stared at her silently. Internally, she was raging, but she would not let that show. She inhaled, locking her emotions away to be dealt with at another time. If Lyra was going to treat her like the leader of their group, if everyone was going to turn to her regardless of her wishes...

Well, then she would make the call.

"You may take the clothes you're wearing but nothing else," she said. To her surprise, her voice was calm. It was as though she was somewhere else and was letting somebody who wasn't Penelope take over her body.

Lyra's eyes widened. "Wh-what?"

"You are no longer welcome here. We have done our best to give you support in your time of need, and you have done nothing but take advantage of us. Leave."

Lyra fell back a step. "But... but the krakens—"

"I didn't say you have to go back to the ocean. Only that you may no longer stay here." Penelope pointed toward the west. "There's a level spot of ground a kilometer away that you can build on."

"But we can't build anything. We've been doing our best; we just don't understand—"

"You have had plenty of opportunity to learn." Penelope folded her arms over her chest, keeping her chin level and her voice low. "We don't exist to serve you. I'm done discussing this."

"Is this about the food?"

Penelope didn't answer. She would not give Lyra a reason to argue back against this. The situation had been getting worse. Around her, her classmates were watching in tense silence. Kaia shifted from foot to foot while the two professors stood at the back of the group, both frowning.

She didn't care if they thought this was a mistake. Penelope was done with it. If the group decided they would allow the mermaids to stay, with no substantial change, then Penelope was gone. She couldn't take this any longer.

"Wait!" Lyra explained, even though Penelope hadn't moved an inch. "We don't know how to survive on the land!"

"Then learn," Penelope replied.

Lyra's shoulders slumped. "But we helped Kaia. We washed the clothes."

Penelope narrowed her eyes, still not budging.

"You can't do this," Lyra spat, her shoulders throwing back now. She tossed her blue-green hair and propped her hands on her hips. "This isn't how things are done in Eldavon. You don't have the authority to cast us out. You need a vote."

"Fine." That was true enough. Penelope whirled, facing her classmates. "Everyone who wants to keep them around—"

"Wait!" Lyra cried again. "You're supposed to use your little ballots. You can't just ask people—they'll feel intimidated."

"Everyone who wants to keep them around, speak now," Penelope said.

Kaia winced, twisting her hands. "I wouldn't feel right kicking them out, Pen. But I agree that something needs to change. Even if we started them off with simple chores around camp, they do that hunting that Lyra has been promising."

"So, you propose they start working around camp and hunting, bringing in food?" Penelope asked.

Kaia nodded.

"And what consequences if they continue to make excuses?"

"We're not making excuses," Lyra whined.

Penelope ignored her. "Should we have a timeline that they have to stick to? The longer they stay here, the more they can claim the hardship of winter to keep leeching off us."

"We're mermaids, not leeches!"

Kaia lifted her hands. "Tomorrow? Either they hunt tomorrow and bring in food, or they leave. That's what I think."

"I thought you were my friend!" Lyra wailed.

Penelope looked at the others. "Does anyone have objections?"

Silence answered her.

"Very well." Penelope turned to Lyra. "You hunt tomorrow and bring in at least enough food to replace what you've carelessly destroyed, or you go."

Lyra's lip trembled, but her expression hardened soon enough. "Fine. Fine, we'll hunt for you and make sure we meet your demands. But we have demands of our own."

Penelope clenched her jaw; she was on the verge of taking back the deal that she had already offered.

"We won't work with that thing," Lyra said, gesturing toward Raven. "We don't have to share clothes, water, or utensils. The diseased monster can have their own so their sickness doesn't spread."

"I have warned you not to speak that way," Penelope growled, her hackles raising.

Lyra tossed her head. "If you think you can force us to break bread with that demon—"

"Say it one more time," Penelope warned. Her dragon claws were poking through, a heat burning in her chest. "Insult my fated mate with one more word. I promise you; I have been civil. Don't push me."

"Fated mate?" Lyra gasped.

Penelope ignored the shocked murmurs from her classmates. No, she and Raven had told no one about them being mates. They wanted time to figure it out themselves first.

It was unfortunate to come out this way, but Penelope didn't have the mental stamina to care. Not when this mermaid princess kept insulting Raven. Everything going down was bad enough, but Penelope was finally pushed too far.

"Nothing more to say?" Penelope demanded.

"I didn't know."

"And that shouldn't have made a difference. I told you from the start, don't insult Raven. Don't call them diseased or a monster. They're a person, a beautiful soul who got caught in something beyond their control. And I am sick and tired of you."

She wanted to say more. But mermaids traded with Eldavon. Eldavon put ships across the ocean, and if Lyra really was a princess, she might have the power to turn their mermaid kingdoms against them.

Penelope bit her tongue, reminding herself that they needed to be smart. That she couldn't jeopardize all of the Kingdom in her fit of temper.

But by the sun, if Lyra said one more thing against Raven...

KAIA FELT the danger in the air. She had been in dangerous situations before. Finnegan had outright tried to kill her once, and she had had to fight him off from harming her friends several times since.

This was a different sort of danger, though. This was the danger of a dragon pushed too far. Someone meant to be an ally on the verge of breaking everything. Not that she blamed Penelope—but this had to stop before it went even further.

Lyra would not back down. Neither was Penelope. Which meant someone else had to do it for them.

Taking a deep breath, Kaia strode forward. Just as Penelope had stepped between Lyra and Herja moments earlier, Kaia now stepped between Penelope and Lyra.

"Pen." Kaia lowered her voice so only Penelope could hear it. "I'll handle this."

"Kaia—"

"I'll handle it. Take Raven somewhere else, calm down, and then when you're ready, we'll talk more. Right now, let me take care of this." Kaia kept her voice gentle but hoped she was still firm enough for Penelope not to argue with her.

Penelope's gaze slid from Lyra to Raven, who stood at the back of the group. She nodded once and headed toward her mate. Herja and Wickham fell into step with her on one side, with Lena and Victor on the other.

Good. Kaia didn't think it was a smart idea for Penelope to be alone right now.

As soon as they were gone, Lyra sniffed. Great big tears welled in her eyes. "Kaia, that's so mean. We've been trying our best to help, but now—"

"Lyra, please. You know that this isn't just because of Penelope," Kaia said sternly.

Lyra closed her mouth and folded her arms.

Adina joined them, standing equal to Kaia. "We're standing with

Penelope and Raven one hundred percent. Also, know that I'm the daughter of King Sydney and Queen Abigail of Eldavon, Lyra. So, I understand the burden of being a princess."

"I'm just concerned for all of you," Lyra said. "You don't know what gorgons are capable of."

"Other than turning people into stone?" Kaia asked.

Lyra opened her mouth and then closed it.

"Raven has taken preventative measures to prevent accidentally turning people into stone," Kaia continued. "Why else do you think they wear the face veil?"

Adina nodded. "You have given us no reason to throw Raven out of our group except insulting them. So now, you have a choice. Accept that Raven is an essential part of our group or do as Penelope told you and leave."

"It's unfathomable that you would rather have a gorgon in your midst than your long-term allies," Lyra insisted.

Adina frowned. She glanced at Kaia, and Kaia nodded once at her. She would take care of this even if it meant arguing in circles. Lyra loved the sound of her own voice, especially when she had something to whine about.

It was an unfortunate truth that the interactions Kaia had been most looking forward to had quickly become the ones she dreaded more than anything else.

"Why is it unfathomable? Is it unfathomable that you would rather be here, with us, than with the krakens?" Kaia asked.

"That's not the same."

"Maybe, but it's an important point," Kaia admitted. "You are the ones that came to us. You were in a dangerous situation and knew we would help you. Why? Because that's what we do. We help people who need it. Including Raven."

Lyra huffed.

Kaia shook her head. Her shoulders and back were tight with frustration, but if she could get things smoothed down and soothe bruised egos, they might start working harmoniously together.

"I can understand your fears," she intoned. "Based on the stories I know, I would be afraid, too. But I know Raven. We all do. They put themselves in harm's way to protect Penelope, Wickham, Herja, Nolen, and me last year."

"Did they?" Lyra asked sarcastically.

"They did—and I'm disappointed that you would think that you have any right to make us go against our core tenants and kick them out," Kaia said. She tried to mimic the way Mama looked when she caused trouble.

Lyra looked ashamed.

"Eldavon doesn't go around banishing people for what they can't control."

"You don't understand about gorgons."

Kaia resisted the urge to roll her eyes. "Frankly, I don't think you do, either."

Lyra stared at her hard, then flipped her hair and shrugged. "I suppose it doesn't matter. Since we either must put up with your demands or starve to death."

"That's not what is happening, and you know it," Kaia said sharply. "You seem to think just because we offer kindness; you can walk all over us. That isn't the case, Lyra. This isn't about you."

She turned and walked away then, having said everything she needed to. The only question was, would the mermaids listen?

CHAPTER
TEN

WICKHAM EYED Penelope and Kaia as he scrubbed the burnt bits of porridge off the bottom of the pot. They worked together to dry and put away all the dishes he had washed but only talked to each other in short, clipped sentences.

Winter had officially fallen. The first snowfall stuck to the ground outside, although as the day warmed up, Wickham figured it would melt before sunset. Still, it represented a change. The frosty air reflected the frostiness that had remained in camp since Penelope had confronted Lyra.

"So... are you and Raven going down to the beach again today?" he asked, trying to ease his heaviness.

Penelope nodded.

"Still seeing the krakens?"

Another nod.

Wickham dumped the water into a bucket and frowned at the burnt bottom of the pot. "Kaia, will you and Nolen be going with them?"

"No."

"Oh? But the krakens seem to be most afraid of Nolen, don't you think—"

"No," Kaia said again.

Wickham poured some fresh water into the pan and started scrubbing it again. Over on the 'laundry' side of camp, a half-dozen mermaids set out the clothes they had just washed. This wasn't the only instance of them showing that they did, in fact, have the skills to care for themselves.

It boiled his blood to realize that the mermaids had been lazing around for no reason and that their excuses about not knowing how to do the work were just excuses. He wished he understood why they would do that. But Lyra still insisted she 'didn't know' and was just a fast learner.

At least the mermaids had finally gone out for their hunt and brought back three adult elk. It was enough meat to last the camp for some time, and Herja could concentrate on bringing in plant-based foods to help stave off scurvy.

Penelope and Raven had remained distant from the others, though. Instead of staying with the other students, they had even built their own tiny log cabin.

And the ice between Kaia and Penelope was also picking at Wickham's consciousness.

He let out an aggravated sigh and straightened. "I think we're going to have to let this pot sit awhile."

"Okay," Kaia said.

Penelope grabbed the last plate and dried it off.

"All right, are you two mad at me or each other?" Wickham demanded, fisting his hands at his sides.

Both girls' heads popped up. Their eyes were both wide and startled.

"What makes you think we're mad at anyone?" Kaia hedged.

Penelope looked up at the sky. "I think it's obvious."

Kaia scowled but shrugged. "I suppose, yeah."

"Why are you two fighting?" Wickham asked, looking between them.

"We're not fighting—not directly, at least," Penelope said, turning her face away.

At this, Kaia snorted. "Not fighting directly? We've been cold and snippy to each other for days, Pen. I'm pretty sure that counts as fighting directly. In fact, I'd say this is the worst fight you, and I have ever had."

Penelope's frown deepened, but her lips twitched. The tension eased from her as she laughed and shook her head, her long braid twitching down her back. "Okay. You've got me there. This is an intense fight for us."

At least they were talking to each other now.

"So, what are you fighting about?" Wickham asked cautiously. He didn't want to set things off—but if he knew anything from his twin brothers' fights, the best way to get over things was to air grievances.

Kaia and Penelope eyed each other warily.

"It's okay if you're not in the right headspace right now—but I think it would be good to talk this through," Wickham said. "It's because of the mermaids and how they react to Raven, right?"

Penelope's face fell into a fierce glower, that she turned on him. "So instead of seeing if we really are in the right headspace, you just push us to it, huh?"

"Pen, please don't snap," Kaia groaned. "Yes. Yes, it's because of Lyra and the mermaids and everything. I would have thought that them pulling their weight would help, but it feels like we've just slapped a band-aid on the—"

"You should have defended Raven more," Penelope interrupted.

Kaia propped her hands on her hips. "I have defended Raven, Pen."

"Not enough. Why would Lyra feel comfortable calling them names around you if—"

"Because Lyra is a self-centered princess who doesn't think about anyone but herself," Kaia interrupted. "I could tell her every second of every day I don't like the way she's talking, and the only way she'd change it is if I was threatening to make her wash her own clothes."

Penelope snorted again.

"I don't like her behavior either. But she and the mermaids have changed their behavior. I'm the only one she listens to, and I have to keep what influence I have," Kaia explained, her shoulders slumping.

Penelope glanced to where Lyra was bundled up next to the fire, playing in it.

"I hate the way she talks about Raven. I do. I've told her as such... but that's one area she doesn't listen to me in." Kaia reached for Penelope's hand. "I don't want her to ruin our friendship."

"I don't, either. I'm sorry, Kaia. It's this situation. I hate it."

Kaia nodded. "There's a lot of tension around here. Maybe we need to have another meeting. Everyone I've talked to have said that they want to call it in and get help from the Institute, but—"

"Wickham!" Victor yelled, bursting out of the trees. "Wickham, we need you!"

⁂

ADINA LEANED HEAVILY on Odele and Herja, blood dripping down her side as they carried her through the forest. Herja's hands were clamped on Adina's side, holding in as much blood as possible.

If it weren't for that injury, they would have flown back—but unfortunately, Herja couldn't figure out how to keep the pressure on Adina's wound while flying on Odele's back.

Tears dripped down her classmates' faces, but Herja forced down the panic that threatened to consume her.

They'd get to camp, and everything would be okay. Wickham was there. West and Ealdwulf were both there.

Adina was going to be okay.

They were all going to be fine.

Her foot caught on some protruding rock from the forest floor, and she stumbled. Her grip on Adina shifted, and her fingers slid—the cloth bunched on the wound slid, too, and Herja's fingers dug into the open injury.

Adina jerked, her head flipping back as she screamed. Odele had to catch her.

"I'm sorry!" Herja panted as she regained her footing. She pressed the cloth back into place and clamped her hand tighter, so she wouldn't slide this time. "I'm sorry."

Adina only sobbed in response.

Soon, Wickham met them, being led by Victor. He took one look at them and made Herja and Odele lay Adina down on the ground. He got to work at once while he spoke over his shoulder.

"We need the professors. I can't deal with this on my own."

"I'll get them," Victor said, but he looked like he was about to fall over, so Herja grabbed his arm, stopping him.

"Get back to camp and tell a witch or dragon to call them using mind-to-mind. We need them as fast as they can get here."

Victor nodded and took off once more.

Odele knelt beside Adina, holding her hand as Wickham worked on her side. There was more blood than in any injury Herja had seen with their classmates before, and she knelt beside Wickham and looked through his bag, pulling out what she knew he would need. He worked silently, his hands passing over the injury to heal it.

All the while, Adina's face grew paler.

It requires a great deal of energy to heal another person. The best doctors knew how to draw energy from outside sources, a 'transfusion' of sorts, from one person to another. Wickham wasn't at that stage, however. He'd be using his own resources, but most of it came from Adina herself.

"Wick," Herja murmured. "You need to stop—she doesn't have enough."

Wickham's hands paused. He looked up at Adina and muttered something under his breath. Then he grabbed the tiny potion bottles he carried with him and alternated between pouring them on the wound and down Adina's throat.

"What even happened?" Wickham demanded.

"Another boar," Odele explained. She stroked Adina's hair from her pale face. "It came out of nowhere. We were just digging up roots when it attacked us. We tried to drive it off, but it was like it deliberately attacked Adina. It threw her into the air and gored her and—"

She choked off.

Herja's throat tightened as the memory of those moments flooded her. It didn't take long, only a few seconds, yet they burned like she had been caught in thick mud for hours, unable to help her friends.

"How bad is it?" Adina asked. "Am I going to die?"

Wickham flinched but shook his head. "Of course not. You'll be back up before you know it. Especially once the professors get here."

His voice was confident and soothing... but Herja could see the tremble in his hands. Her stomach flipped when she dared to look at the injury he was cleaning and treating. It was terrible, worse than she had thought. Adina was opened up from hip to armpit. Her skin flapped loosely on either side, and there was so much blood.

Herja turned her face away again, fighting not to vomit. She realized Odele was looking at her and fought to slip on a mask, so she wouldn't show how worried she was.

Wickham's skills weren't enough. Adina needed to get back to the Institute. Otherwise, she didn't stand a chance.

CHAPTER
ELEVEN

THE PORTAL-MIRROR WAS TUCKED into a cave, safe from being accidentally destroyed. It was only a short distance from where the professors had set camp. With the help of the two professors, Wickham got Adina's bleeding under control so they could move her again.

It went without saying that she would go back to the Institute. The students made a stretcher, and the six dragons carried her to the mirror while West went on ahead to activate it.

The mirror was huge, wide enough for three people to walk through at once. The frame was made of obsidian, and the metals inside rippled with images of the Institute on the other side. Wickham wanted to go through, not just to monitor Adina and to hear updates about her at all times. But because the thought of a bed and a hot meal was so tempting.

The whole situation here at the sea camp just seemed to have gotten worse.

"All right, so we've got Professors Delphine and Farrow waiting to take the stretcher," West said as he took the head of the stretcher. "So, you don't need to come through."

The students nodded. Ealdwulf was back at the camp still. He'd stay with them until West returned with news about Adina's condition.

Right now, she was alert and seemed like she wasn't in too much pain, although her face was still pale.

"Odele?" Adina called.

Odele was already near the front of the stretcher and looked down, blinking rapidly.

"I want you to stay. Here, I mean, with the others." Adina reached up and took Odele's hand. "I'll be fine."

"But..." Odele bit her lip, then sighed. "If you're sure..."

"I am."

Wickham glanced away as Odele pressed a kiss to Adina's lips. She stepped back and West backed through the mirror. The dragons released the stretcher one by one, and Adina disappeared through the mirror.

To the Institute, Wickham reminded himself. *Where she'll get the medical care she needs.*

Odele stood twisting her hands as the mirror faded to black again. Nolen went to his twin sister and put a comforting arm around her, while Xena and Vera sighed heavily and headed back to camp.

Herja stepped up to Wickham and slid her hand into his. "Are you okay?"

Wickham nodded. "Yeah. I think so. I'm just thinking about when we were in the Silent Marshes and even last year when we were always getting soaked through and running out of herbs... We've lived through some major crises already."

"We have," Herja agreed.

Nolen and Odele left the cave. Wickham and Herja still stood there, looking at the mirror. All it would take was Wickham holding his hand out to it, and the mirror would activate again and allow him to leave.

"We don't have to wait until we're in crisis to return home this time," he said. "But there just feels like there's so much more holding me here than being unable to leave. We've already faced some major injuries already. I don't want to leave only to hear someone else got hurt when I could have helped."

Herja tugged on his hand lightly, pulling him away.

Wickham sighed as he followed. Outside, the air was crisp. The ground was wet with melted snow, but the sun shone brightly, warming his face.

"There are always dangers in these camps," Herja said as they walked toward camp. "It's not common for dangerous animals to be in the bay. It's why the Institute chose it for the students' final quest."

Wickham sighed. "Meaning that once again, we're the group that faces more than we were meant to," he murmured, more to himself than to Herja. "Once again, we have to go through unforeseen dangers. Why can't the Institute just send us a few more adults? Some witches to cast the boars away entirely?"

"We haven't asked for help," Herja pointed out.

Wickham shrugged. "Maybe they should do it without us having to ask. Maybe we've already gone through situations where we can't ask, so now, when we can, it still feels like we can't."

"We're all tired," Herja said.

"I know."

"Maybe it would be better if we asked for help. Maybe we don't have to give up our quest. But maybe we can get the Institute to send some people to handle the mermaids, and we can have our camp back," Herja continued. She straightened slightly; her expression was lighter. "Even with them helping around camp more—"

"It's still a lot of work."

Herja nodded. "And a lot of responsibility. Responsibility, I, for one, am not happy about having. But there's a middle ground between keeping the mermaids with us and giving up entirely."

Wickham tiredly nodded.

"I asked Ealdwulf if this was the same sort of situation as we had with the Chameleon Sprites. You know, where the agreement differed from what we knew."

"Yeah. And?"

"He said it wasn't. Promised it wasn't." Herja glanced up at the sky, frowning. "And I think I believe him. Row would have told me this time, and the Headmasters know not to throw us into these things anymore."

Wickham couldn't help but sigh deeply at this news. While it assured him that, on the one hand, they would get help if they asked, it didn't help him feel any better. Once again, something strange was happening with their year.

He felt very old for only seventeen years. Too much was happening, it seemed. Every year they went through something new, and he was tiring of it.

But they still needed him at camp.

They arrived back shortly. Everyone was gathered around the fire, the mood subdued. Kaia stood as they approached, twisting her hands.

"Is Adina going to be ok?" she asked.

Herja answered, "I'm sure she will, now that she's at the Institute."

"She seemed more comfortable before she went through the mirror," Wickham said. "And Herja's right; she'll get the care she needs now she's back at the Institute."

"I just don't get it," Kaia said as she sank back down. She rubbed her eyes. "We've been walking all over the place and have seen no sign of boars, sows, or any of them. So how did this happen? And why did it attack Adina?"

"I don't think we'll ever know the answer to that," Penelope said.

Lyra snorted and shot Raven a pointed look but twisted her head when Penelope looked at her. Wickham glared at the mermaid. While they were acting more cordial toward Raven, they were only doing so because Penelope had threatened to kick them out.

But Herja's idea of having the Institute send people here to take care of the mermaids while the students could focus on what their year was supposed to be? Now that sounded good.

"The point is, Adina had made it back to the Institute," Wickham said as he came to sit near Kaia at the fire. "And we know that there is another boar in the area, and it will attack without provocation. So, it's time we come up with a plan for how to proceed."

"Don't forget the krakens," Lyra added. "I went to check the beach this morning, and one of them nearly beached itself trying to get me."

"Yes," Herja said, striding forward to stand in the center of the circle. "We need to decide what we're doing. Staying, going, or something else entirely."

70

AS EXPECTED, Lyra protested as soon as Herja suggested they leave. Rather than trying to soothe her—or allowing Kaia to do so—Herja cut in amidst Lyra's wails to assure her they wouldn't be abandoning the mermaids.

"If we as students choose to leave, the Institute will send other people, adults who are experienced enough to take care of the situation, to help you," she said, keeping her tone flat. "You won't be left to starve over the winter and will probably have a better situation."

Lyra folded her arms, not like she was happy with this answer, but also not able to argue against it.

"We're going to have another vote," Herja said. "But first, I want everyone to take some time to think of in-between possibilities. It doesn't have to be just that we leave or stay. We can call in some help and have a new store of food brought in. We could ask the military to help drive the krakens away."

Penelope nodded as she stood up next to Herja. "Herja's making a good point. We don't have to see our options in a binary light. I, for one, think it will also be a good idea for us to state our votes verbally. I want to know what everyone is thinking."

Herja nodded her agreement. While she thought, for the most part, it was important to have anonymity so that people were free to vote the way they wanted, in this case, they needed to have more of a discussion rather than just blind voting.

"What about us?" Lyra asked. "Do we get a vote?"

"No," Penelope said without looking at her.

Herja touched her elbow. "Pen. I understand your feelings, but we could use their input on possibilities."

"But they don't get to vote on what we do," Penelope said.

Herja nodded, accepting that. She turned to Lyra. "If you have any thoughts on possibilities that we can do, we would like to hear them. However, the vote is about what we as students will do, which you don't have a say in."

Lyra looked irritated but nodded.

"One more thing," Herja said, looking around at her classmates. "Regardless of what the vote says, this isn't an all-or-nobody situation. If you want to go home, you are well within your rights to go home, regardless of what anyone else does."

Nods answered her.

She took a seat again and sighed. "All right. So, does anyone have anything they want to say? Suggestions to make?"

The voting was a long, arduous process. Everyone had an opinion, even if they didn't speak up. So Herja eventually had to ask each person individually what their thoughts were as they were speaking. Ealdwulf was the only one who refused to contribute, although Herja would have liked the professor to give his opinion.

In the end, they divided the group evenly into three sections. Wickham, Lena, Penelope, and Odele all wanted to return to the Institute and call it a year. The training this year would be more successful in a stable environment, allowing them to build on the skills they gained in the past.

Despite feeling like it would be good to focus on her learning, Herja disagreed. Nolen, Xena, and Jalene agreed with her. They wanted to tough it out and spend the year as they were supposed to. Only to have another camp set up by the Institute to take care of the mermaids so that Lyra and her people could be more comfortable without the tension between the students who didn't know how to take care of them.

Meanwhile, Kaia, Victor, Icarus, and Vera would give it a month or two, provided they caught the boar that attacked Adina. They wanted to set up the mermaids with plenty of food and housing and put together safeties against the krakens. For them, it wasn't about what the students needed or could get but about setting the mermaids up for success over the winter.

In the end, with the three groups evenly split, the deciding vote was Raven.

Herja couldn't help but note the anxiety on Lyra's face as everyone turned to Raven.

"I think... that at the time being, with the attack on Adina, emotions are running high," they said slowly as they rubbed their hands together. "I think I would like to take a week to do heavy preparations. Gather as much food and firewood as possible, and once that week is over, see how well we're doing."

Herja nodded and turned to the four who wanted to leave. "Is that going to work for you?"

They looked weary but nodded one by one. Herja sighed as she rubbed the back of her neck. All right. One week, then, and we'll reassess. Now dragons, let's figure out how to get that boar."

CHAPTER

TWELVE

KAIA HAD BEEN STANDING with the cooking pot in her hands, staring at the disastrous scene before her, for at least five minutes before Raven came out of the house.

Raven gasped and ran to Kaia. They drew up beside her, then stopped. Kaia couldn't bring herself to turn to her companion. Couldn't do anything besides look on with numb horror.

The sky was alive with a frenzy of feathers, a tempest of squawking and screeching. Seagulls of various sizes swarmed the area, their wings beating frantically as they grabbed strips of meat and bolted. Small creatures, everything from foxes to stoats, scurried over the campsite, fighting over a scrap here and there. Their lithe bodies wove through the debris, chowing down on a veritable feast.

"What happened?" Raven asked, their voice subdued.

"I don't know," Kaia replied as she stared at the open hole that had been their food storehouse. "It's gone. All our food... gone."

The animals still fought over the dried and cured meat they had stored, but even the nuts, the roots, everything... It was gone.

All their hard work. And nothing to show for it except the squabbling of animals.

Kaia had been the first one awake and started a fire for breakfast.

She hadn't heard the noise until she stepped outside and closed the door behind her.

First, she tried to run the scavengers off, thinking they might salvage something. It was clear that everything had been damaged, and she had no desire to tell the other students.

"Didn't the cellar have spells on it?" Raven asked.

Kaia wished they would be quiet. The more they talked, the more she had to process the situation. The more she processed, the more she felt—and the more she wanted to collapse and sob.

"It did," Kaia said. "I don't know what happened. I just came out here, and this was happening. We're going to starve."

Raven turned to her and put their hands on her shoulders bracingly. "No. We will not starve. We will go back to the Institute and let the adults take care of the situation."

"We are adults," Kaia mumbled.

"No, we're not. We're still teenagers. And this is exactly why we have the mirror to take us back to the Institute, Kaia. Who could have seen this coming?"

Kaia didn't answer. No-one. Of course, they couldn't have seen this coming... but it didn't stop her from feeling utterly defeated.

Raven headed back into the cabin, and they must have told everyone else because the other students came stumbling out shortly after. Despite the cries of disbelief and the postulation as to what could have happened, everyone ended up quiet and somber. Kaia felt like this was somehow her fault, that if she had voted the same as Penelope and they had left, they wouldn't face such a disaster.

"Are you okay?" Nolen asked her quietly as he stepped up next to her.

Kaia turned and buried her face into his shirt, breathing his scent in deeply. Having the solid warmth of her mate nearby helped a bit, but this year was a bust.

"I'm okay," Kaia murmured. "Just angry and disappointed."

Odele informed the mermaids what happened, and the beautiful, glittering women left their cabin to view the scene with expressions of shock. Lyra pressed both her hands to her mouth.

"Did someone attack us?" one mermaid asked, sounding utterly bewildered.

Herja had been hunting around the site and pointed out wide trails on the sand. They were covered in a thick goo of some sort as though giant snails had crossed the way. Snails, or...

"Krakens," Herja said grimly. "Look at the beach. Those tracks look just like an octopus'. The krakens must have pulled themselves up the shore to destroy the food stores."

"But why?" Kaia and Lyra both burst out together.

Lyra shook her head. "Krakens don't come this far ashore."

"And if they had come up, why would they just attack the food cellar, not our cabins?" Kaia asked. "And why didn't we hear anything? It's like there are silencing charms on the cabins."

Herja flashed her a warning look, one that she didn't get—until she caught sight of how Lyra was glaring at Raven. Kaia's stomach dropped. No. No, Lyra would not blame this on Raven! Kaia ground her teeth together, a whole new suspicion bursting into her mind.

Mermaids had magic. If anyone knew how to set the scene to make it look as though the krakens had attacked them, it would be Lyra. And while Kaia couldn't see a reason for it, Lyra's obvious hatred of Raven might just give her a motive.

She inhaled sharply as Lyra opened her mouth. "It doesn't matter, though, does it?"

Lyra gave her a startled look.

"It's happened, and the krakens are the only ones that would have reason to do this," Kaia continued. "But it's clear we only have one option. We must go back to the Institute."

Ealdwulf nodded. "I think that is how it must be," he said, proving Kaia's point entirely.

For the professors who didn't interject unless they had reason to, this was reason to. Some of the pressure weighing down on Kaia's chest eased. She wanted to go home. She was tired of being here, of fighting through all of what was happening.

Yes, she had put in a lot of effort. Yes, she had been pushing to keep moving through all of this, but she was tired of pushing, of searching for the bright side, of overseeing all the domestic labor of the camp. She wanted to sleep in her own bed; she wanted to eat something that she didn't have to make and didn't have to clean up after.

She wanted to see her family, wanted to have time to read or swim or play after lessons. And now she was in a position where she, at last, had no more reasons to fight against it. How was it such a relief to have circumstances state that she no longer had to make the choice? Maybe it was because she had been choosing based on what she thought she needed to do, rather than what she actually wanted.

But even as this relief swept over her, Lyra made a small, quiet noise. As Kaia turned to her, she was shocked to see the mermaid's eyes well with tears.

"But what will become of us?" Lyra asked quietly.

⚓

PENELOPE SIGHED HEAVILY. As much as she felt for Lyra and the mermaids in their situation, hadn't they already talked about this? While Kaia twisted her hands, looking almost ashamed of herself, Penelope just wanted to snap—*you're coming with us.*

But that wouldn't be diplomatic.

And if there was one thing she had learned throughout this semester so far, she lacked diplomacy. If she was going to be part of the military, though, she needed to learn how to be diplomatic. The last thing they needed was someone who would leap to anger or violence... something Penelope understood she had been doing more and more of late.

It would be easy to let the others deal with Lyra, to be the diplomatic ones there. But Penelope cleared her throat, bringing everyone's attention to her. She had caused some damage already to their relationship. Maybe this was a chance for her to make it up.

"You can either come with us, or you can stay here, and we'll send you aid," she said, keeping her voice even and her tone soft. "I know it's not a simple choice."

"An impossible choice, you mean," Lyra argued. "If we stay, the krakens will come after us again. And if we go, we'll be forced to spend who knows how long away from our sea."

Penelope nodded once; it was perfectly reasonable to have those worries, after all. "Another thing you could do is to come with us and then arrange with the Institute and Crown to get you back to your major cities. I think it's obvious now, though, that we students can't stay here."

"But we still won't be near the sea until we're transported back," Lyra argued.

"I'm sorry," Herja said as she came to stand with Penelope, "I'm going to have to agree with Penelope. You either stay or come with us. If you stay, you either accept aid from the Crown or you don't. If you come with us, you either negotiate transportation back to the sea or you don't. Your choice to make."

Lyra folded her arms as she chewed her lip.

Penelope turned to the other students. "Let's get our stuff together. We'll head out in two hours."

"Two hours isn't long enough to decide," Lyra protested.

"It's long enough for you to decide to stay or to go," Penelope replied. "And once you've made that choice, the others will come naturally after."

She turned on her heel and headed back toward the cabin. This time when she entered it, she could still hear the murmur of voices combined with the raucous calls of the animals. So why hadn't they been able to hear it before?

She had just gotten her bedroll put together when Raven came into the cabin. They organized their things. They wore a scarf today, the shape of their nose pressing against the face veil.

Penelope studied what she could see of their profile, wishing she could see more. So much could be said between people in minute facial expressions, and it felt like she and Raven had this enormous block between them.

"Did I overstep out there?" Penelope finally asked. "I went on and on about not wanting to be the de facto leader, and now..."

"Professor Ealdwulf is talking with Lyra, explaining the various possibilities he already discussed with the Institute," Raven replied. "The others are gathering up the food scraps so they can take them elsewhere in case the mermaids wish to stay."

Penelope wrinkled her nose. "They should prioritize themselves, not the mermaids. Or maybe they should clean up camp before it brings in bigger predators. I don't know. Are you okay?"

Raven laughed softly. "I'm fine."

"And will you be okay if the mermaids come back to the Institute with us?"

Raven's hands stilled for a moment, and then they shook their head. "I will not say where they can and cannot go, especially in these circumstances. Besides, we won't have to deal with them so... intimately anymore."

"That's true," Penelope agreed.

At the Institute, they would have the professors to deal with the mermaids. It wouldn't be on the students' shoulders anymore.

"And with any luck, when we're with people who are better equipped to handle all of this, we'll be able to find out more about what the mermaids know of gorgons," Raven whispered.

Penelope nodded, but internally her heart dropped. That was right. The Crown would want to talk to the mermaids more about why they were so against gorgons. It wouldn't just be the Institute. The professors there, the Headmasters, Penelope understood and trusted.

She trusted the kings and queens, too, but not on a personal level. She didn't know them, didn't know what they already thought about Raven.

What if the mermaids turned the Crown against Raven for being a gorgon? What if Lyra convinced Adina's parents that Raven was the reason their daughter was so badly injured?

What if this was the start of something terrible?

CHAPTER
THIRTEEN

ULTIMATELY, it took them five hours to get ready to leave. It was partly because of Lyra's overall behavior, trying to convince them all to stay and just move camp. Wickham wasn't sure if she understood how much work it was to build their cabins or if she was being willfully ignorant.

It was a relief when the group finally got to the cave where the mirror was. Wickham rubbed the back of his neck, putting his long silver hair into a bun for the day.

He was looking forward to a proper bath. Out of all the benefits that being back at the Institute would give them, being clean was at the top of his list. That, and being able to have regular updates as to Adina's condition. However, he didn't consider that a luxury.

"Are you certain this is safe?" Lyra asked, peering at the mirror doubtfully.

The image within was... stormy today. It wasn't a clear image like when they sent Adina through.

"It's perfectly safe," Ealdwulf assured her. "The ripples you're seeing are because of the extra power being fed into the mirror, so we can all go through easily."

Lyra wrinkled her nose but turned to Kaia. "Please come with me. I don't want to go through by myself."

That was understandable. As Wickham watched the image waver, he wasn't sure he wanted to go through it alone. He hadn't ever moved through a mirror-portal like this before. He'd used portals in their second year with the Chameleon Sprites, but those had been quite different.

"Of course," Kaia agreed.

Lyra looped her arm through Kaia's and clung to her tightly as they approached the mirror. Just before they stepped in, Lyra hesitated. She reached out to touch the obsidian frame, then let out a heavy breath.

"All right. Let's do this," she said, sounding like she was preparing for battle.

Kaia tugged on Lyra's arm, and the two stepped through together. Next to go were the rest of the mermaids, and finally, the students moved through.

Wickham lingered at the back with Herja and Penelope, watching everyone else go through. Once they, too, went through the mirror, Wickam stepped up to it. He was the last student here. But he hesitated. He couldn't stay here by himself, he knew that, but there was still some part of him that wondered if they had made a mistake with this choice.

"Are you all right, Wickham?" Ealdwulf asked.

He turned back to the professor. "I guess part of me feels like giving up makes me a failure. Not anyone else. Just me. Even though I want nothing more than to go back to the Institute."

"Why would you alone be a failure while the others aren't?" Ealdwulf asked, his brow furrowed.

Wickham smiled wryly as he lifted his hands. "Because I'm kind of the doctor. I know I don't have the full training, but even in our first year, I've been the one taking care of injuries. As soon as I decide to leave, what are they supposed to do?"

"You weren't the first to decide to leave," Ealdwulf pointed out. "And West and I have had more medical training than you."

"That doesn't change the way I feel," Wickham replied with a shrug.

Ealdwulf nodded slowly, then gave him a small smile. "You have elected to prioritize your health and safety, Wickham. If you feel like the health of the entire group is on your shoulders, who is responsible for your health?"

Wickham opened his mouth and closed it again.

"You and your classmates have proven yourselves many times over already," Ealdwulf said, his expression softening. "Why else would we have given the choice to you? You voted to come here, and you voted to leave. There is nothing wrong with making sure that you take care of not only your physical but mental health. We are not meant to solve all our problems on our own."

Wickham considered Ealdwulf's words. Knowing that the students were already so highly thought of certainly helped with these feelings of being disappointed in himself. He'd have to remember this, especially in the future.

With one last grateful smile at Ealdwulf, Wickham stepped through the portal.

And instantly knew something was wrong.

It felt as though he was being buffeted through monstrous waves. Water spilled into his lungs, even when he closed his mouth. Something hard slammed into his side, but instead of air driving from him, it was nothing but liquid. A tearing feeling ripped through his body. His limbs were being pulled apart, and his skull was split in two.

He kicked wildly as a single point of light appeared before him. He clawed through thick mud as it invaded his nose and ears.

Then the pain became too much. His eyes rolled to the back of his head, and he knew no more.

WATER PASTED Herja's hair to her head. She panted, trying desperately to get in air, even though she knew she had air all around her. Her arms wrapped around Wickham's unconscious body. He was likewise soaked through, but blood trickled from his nose.

"You're all fine," Lyra sighed dramatically as she flipped her green-blue hair over her shoulder. It seemed to have grown several inches from the time she stepped through the portal to now. "You're just disoriented a little, is all."

Herja bent her ear closer to Wickham. He was breathing, though shallowly. "He's hurt."

Lyra craned her neck to peer at Wickham. She hummed as she shrugged. "I'll have a doctor look at him. He shouldn't have waited so long to come through the portal. Or just waited a few more minutes; he's only in that shape because it was closing when he entered."

A growl rose in Herja's throat, but she repressed it as they looked around. All her classmates were here with her in a large, sand-colored room. The floor was covered in an intricate mosaic, while the walls appeared to be sandstone. In the center of the room was an obsidian mirror, like the one that they had entered.

It was a trap. Somehow, it had been a trap from the start.

All around them were mermaids. Tall, powerfully muscular, and wearing leather and copper armor. They carried curved swords and massive spears, and each one looked on at the students with utterly blank expressions.

Kaia stumbled to her feet, turning to face Lyra. She appeared to be the driest of the students—perhaps because she went through with Lyra?

"What did you do?" Kaia rasped. "Where are we?"

"I merely put a minor glitch in the portal's magic," Lyra replied sweetly.

"Where are we?" Kaia repeated.

Lyra opened her arms, spinning slightly on the spot. "This is the mermaid kingdom of Ylliatia. My home. You should feel very honored, as we never have land-goers in our cities. However, you are special, Kaia. And you will learn more about the mermaid way of life than you ever could on land."

Penelope pulled herself to her feet. She was even more soaked than Wickham, although not as much as Raven. "Why have you done this?

We were perfectly willing to give you aid, Lyra. Why did you kidnap us all?"

"Kidnap is so infantile. I prefer to think of it as taking you hostage," Lyra replied.

A sick feeling sank into the pit of Herja's stomach. Hostages. So, Lyra was hoping to force Eldavon to... what? Give her something? Do something for her?

"What do you want?" Herja demanded.

Lyra only smirked at her.

"You set this up," Nolen accused. He wrapped his arms around Kaia and pulled her protectively to him. "You've been targeting our food stores from the start. You weren't incompetent; you just wanted to force a situation where we'd bring you through the mirror. So how did you get the krakens to attack you?"

"The krakens attacked without provocation," Lyra replied, as though they would believe her.

Penelope shook her head, her red braid twisting like a drowned rat. "What do you want from Eldavon?"

"That is not really your concern," Lyra replied. "You will be treated with dignity and kindness so long as you are here. I have no intention of threatening you with harm so long as you obey our laws."

Herja really did growl this time. "No? Then why take us at all."

"Eldavon will pay handsomely for your return... and for that, all I need is to keep you here until they give me what I want."

Herja looked over her shoulder at the obsidian mirror again. What happened to Professor Ealdwulf? Had he been left behind, or was he sent to the Institute? Or... or had he been in the mirror when the portal closed? Was he lost?

Lyra spread her arms to the students as they all started to protest and argue. "No doubt you are feeling shocked and overwhelmed at the situation. I will give you all time to recover. Take them all to comfortable quarters," she ordered at one guard over her shoulder, then smiled at where Raven still kneeled on the floor. "Except them."

Penelope snarled aloud and sped back to Raven. The rest of the students closed ranks around them, except Herja where she still held

Wickham's unconscious form. His eyes were moving beneath his lids. That was a good sign, right?

"Are you going to send Raven home?" Herja asked, praying to the stars she was right. "There's no point in having hostages if the Crown doesn't know where we are. So, it'd make sense to send Raven back to the Institute. Especially as you don't want a gorgon here."

Lyra turned to her and crouched so they were at eye level. "If I did, would you accept I would send your friend through to the Institute, and not drown them somewhere in the ocean?"

Herja flinched. No. No, she really wouldn't trust Lyra to do any such thing.

"That's what I thought," Lyra said.

"You will not harm my mate," Penelope growled. Smoke was hissing out of her mouth and throat.

Lyra waved a careless hand toward her. "Calm down, Pen. Hostages are no good to me dead and I know I would have to kill you if I were to do anything to the gorgon. But I can't have them wandering my city. The rest of you are free to explore as you like. The gorgon, however, will be locked up."

Penelope hissed again.

Wickham groaned, pulling Herja's attention to him. His eyes started to pinch and relax, as though he was simultaneously trying to peek through his lashes and block out the light. Herja stroked his hair from his face. The nosebleed had stopped, too, although his nose looked puffy and bruised.

"The gorgon will be shown mercy because they are your mate, Penelope," Lyra continued. "But it's as much for their wellbeing to keep them locked away. After all, I may be a princess, but I cannot guarantee my every order will be followed."

Herja looked up again. From where she was, she couldn't see Penelope's face, but the other students were glancing at each other with uncertain looks.

"Take them first to the chambers set aside for the gorgon," Lyra ordered the guard. "Then take the rest of them to their quarters."

She turned and swept away, despite Kaia and Penelope both shouting after her.

Herja couldn't care less that Lyra was leaving. Wickham was moving a little more again, and so long as Raven was safe, they could figure out what to do to improve the situation later.

"Wick, I'm going to have to carry you," she said aloud, hefting him into her arms. Even though Wickham was always a little slender and small compared to the others in their year, she still grunted as she stood.

Nolen stepped toward them. "I can take him when you get tired."

Herja shook her head. "Stay with Penelope and Raven. They need the backup more than me."

Odele and Xena were already flanking the pair, with Icarus and Jalene behind them and Kaia standing before them. Nolen took a long look at them and shook his head.

"You need help, too."

The guards circled behind the group while one of them opened a door and bowed, gesturing through. "If you will follow me."

Slowly, the students started forward. As they did so, Herja and Penelope's gazes met. And Herja could see that Penelope was just as lost and afraid as she was.

CHAPTER

FOURTEEN

KAIA TWISTED her hands as she looked around the elaborate waiting room she was standing in. Though there were several stately chairs, she couldn't bring herself to sit.

How had they gotten here? Even though two days had passed without sunlight, they still calculated time with the light and dark cycles from the glow stones. She still couldn't come to terms with it.

So many lies. And for what purpose?

Lyra told the truth about one thing at least. The chambers the students had been given were comfortable. It was an enormous apartment, much like the dorms back at the Institute. Only here, each of the teens had their own elaborate room. They were all decorated the same, with a queen-sized bed in the center, surrounded by filmy curtains in shades of silver and black.

Each room also had a sitting area, a library, a writing desk, and whatever arts and crafts someone could ask for. Anything they wanted, they were given. So Kaia didn't feel as though she was in danger here. At least, not as though Lyra was going to hurt or kill them.

Ironic how the mermaids had succeeded in what Odentia and Finnegan had failed to do all this time—take the fourth-year students prisoner.

She was pulled out of her thoughts as a great double door carved out of coral opened. Two guards entered and stood on either side of the door as Lyra stepped in.

The mermaid princess wore a shimmering rose dress today. It hugged her body and was split up to the thigh. Kaia blushed at how much skin she had exposed. Though Eldavon cared little about what people wore most of the time, she thought the mermaids thought even less of clothes.

Unlike dragons, who had special spells put on their clothing so that it transferred with them when they shifted from one form to the next, mermaids simply didn't wear clothing when they took their finned forms into the ocean.

Kaia found it very interesting, in the same way she found all differences in culture interesting. That didn't mean she was any more comfortable with nudity.

"Would you like to go for a walk through the gardens?" Lyra asked, then paused and cocked her head. "You're uncomfortable."

Kaia cleared her throat and gestured at the dress. "It's very... um... well, it's very revealing according to Eldavon standards."

"Ah." Lyra looked down at herself. "And you land-goers are uncomfortable with your bodies."

"No, it's just that we see our bodies differently from you. That doesn't mean we're uncomfortable with our bodies. Just that it's different."

Lyra smiled. "But you are uncomfortable."

Kaia wasn't sure how to respond to that. She had a feeling that no matter what she said, Lyra would only take it as an opportunity to debate her. Besides, she wasn't wildly uncomfortable. Just unused to it.

"That's not what I came to talk to you about," she said finally.

"Shall we go to the gardens?" Lyra asked.

Kaia nodded. It felt like another delaying tactic to her, but again, it was something she had a feeling Lyra would just argue with her about. Lyra led her back down a corridor, the guards following behind. Finally, they came to the gardens.

Kaia had seen nothing as beautiful ever before. The greens were more vibrant, and there were flowers of every color. She had always thought the atrium at the Institute was beautiful, but this... this was magnificent. A vast dome arched overhead, with vines growing up their sides, and it was at least as wide as the entire palace complex.

Cascading fountains danced gracefully every few feet, their soothing melodies echoing through the air. Sparkling waterfalls tumbled down moss-covered rocks, which were every hue and shade of gemstone Kaia had heard of—even more.

"Do you like it?" Lyra said in her giggling voice.

"Do I?" Kaia said, mesmerized as they walked through the garden. The perfumed air made her feel giddy and relaxed all at once. "It's... it's amazing."

She stopped near a wide pond. A dozen mermaids sat on the other side of the pond, talking with each other. Vibrant fish basked near the surface, their long flowing fins arching gracefully. They looked like a rainbow, with so many colors and brightness she couldn't name them all.

"Here," Lyra said, wading into the pond. One of the larger fish swam toward her and she scooped it into her arms, lifting it gently from the water.

Kaia opened her mouth to protest, but even as she watched, the vibrant fish wriggled and squirmed. The colorful scales were replaced by muted skin tones, and the gigantic eyes darkened and grew lashes around them. In seconds, a baby lay gurgling in Lyra's arms.

Lyra waded back out of the pond and passed the baby to Kaia. Kaia gaped as the little one grinned toothlessly and kicked both feet.

"You look startled," Lyra laughed. "But we are mermaids. All our young take this form."

Kaia cradled the baby against her chest as the baby cooed. "I didn't know. So these... they're babies?"

"Yes. They're having their water time," Lyra answered and waved to the mermaids across the pond. "They're mothers."

Kaia looked at the mermaids again. One of them was particularly watching them with a worried expression. That must be this little mermaid's mother. She carefully handed the baby back to Lyra, who slid the baby back into the water. It wiggled and turned back into the brightly colored fish.

"I have something else to show you." Lyra continued.

They made their way to a large glass panel in the dome. As Kaia drew close, she saw movement in the water beyond. Lyra waved her hand over the panel, and an image came into clear focus.

Stone towers being torn apart by krakens. Their long, muscular tentacles wrapped around the buildings, crushing them. They tore the towers up from their bases like they were uprooting a tree.

"I evacuated those areas just this morning before the surrounding shields failed," Lyra said grimly. "We had to give up some of the city to protect the rest. But the krakens are relentless in their attacks. They will come after the next section as soon as they're done with that property."

Kaia opened her mouth, then closed it again. The krakens were maintaining their attacks on the mermaids? Even now?

"Our libraries were the first section we lost," Lyra explained. "So much knowledge and history, just gone."

"What is going on, exactly?" Kaia demanded. She turned to Lyra, and her brows pinched together.

Lyra's expression was more serious than Kaia had ever seen it before. "The kraken's attack on us at your campsite was genuine, Kaia. We fled them when they destroyed our village. I was hoping to get help. Instead, my hand was forced."

"But what—"

"Months ago, the krakens started their first attacks. Ever since then, we have been under siege. And it has cost us dearly," Lyra replied.

Kaia shivered as she turned back to watch the krakens destroying the towers.

"They killed my mother in the first attack," Lyra said, and her voice shook. "So there's something else I lied to you about. I'm not a princess at all. I'm the queen."

"The queen," Kaia repeated.

Lyra nodded. "Everything I've tried to do has failed. I didn't want to lie to you and your friends. But I couldn't just trust you with the truth, not when it would render us vulnerable."

"Eldavon would help, though," Kaia protested.

Lyra laughed. "Help. Yes, they would help. By bringing all of my people to their land-buildings. By cutting us off from the sea. And then what? We do not belong on the land, Kaia. And you and your friends showed exactly what 'help' would look like."

Kaia stared at her, uncertain of what she was saying. Was she angry at them for demanding that the mermaids pull their weight at the camp? Did she think the students should have waited on them hand and foot?

"I don't understand what we did wrong," Kaia said.

Lyra smiled, but it was a bitter smile full of anger. "And that is exactly why we can't trust you."

"We can't figure out how to act better if you don't tell us what we did wrong."

"Am I supposed to spell it out for you?"

Kaia bit back the desire to shout at her. "Actually, yes. None of us are trained to be diplomats. None of us know anything about mermaids except what we've learned from previous years. I thought that the relationship between mermaids and Eldavon was good."

Lyra folded her arms.

"I don't understand what you're so angry with us about," Kaia continued. "I—"

A guard hurried up beside the two of them, interrupting. She bowed toward Lyra. "Your grace. The turquoise dragon is causing them problems again."

Penelope. Kaia's heart dropped as Lyra swept off, and she hurried after. What had Penelope gotten herself into this time?

⁂

SEVERAL GUARDS HAD her pinned down, and arms twisted behind her back. Penelope snarled as she fought against them. Anger flowed through her. And the only reason she didn't take her dragon form was because she didn't want to accidentally hurt people who were just doing their job.

Apparently, despite Lyra stating that they could go wherever they wanted, Penelope could no longer visit Raven.

Footsteps sounded and Lyra approached, an annoyed expression on her face. "What is going on here?"

"The dragon was trying to go see the gorgon," one guard said.

Penelope twisted, snapping at this guard's wrist.

"Stop it," a familiar voice cried. Kaia.

What was Kaia doing with Lyra? Didn't she understand the mermaid had set this all up? It was all a ploy, and playing nice with Lyra was only going to put them in a worse predicament!

Lyra glared down at Penelope. "Let her up."

The guards moved aside, seemingly reluctant.

Penelope sprang to her feet and stepped down the corridor to where Raven was being held. The guards blocked her way with their spears and Penelope whirled on Lyra.

"I want to see my mate."

Lyra's face was blank. I have decided that it is not conducive to allow you to go to the gorgon continually. They are poisoning your mind, Penelope."

"You can't be serious," Kaia protested.

"I am. I know that this whole business about the gorgon being your friends' mate was manufactured so that the gorgon—"

"Raven," Penelope snarled, clenching her fists. "Their name is Raven, and the only one manufacturing anything is *you*. If you don't let me go to my mate, I will not hold back."

Even if she didn't know what that meant... Penelope glared at the mermaid. All she really knew was that there was no way she was going to sit around twiddling her thumbs when her mate was locked away. For all she knew, this sudden decision she could not see Raven any longer was because Lyra had done something to Raven.

The thought made Penelope's blood run cold.

Lyra inhaled deeply. "Raven, then. A gorgon doesn't have a fated mate, Penelope. Clearly, you are young and easily influenced—"

"Don't even try," Penelope warned. Her skin prickled as it took on the turquoise shimmer of her scales. "I know Raven is my mate. I have the star threads. I felt the stars bless our union. You aren't going to gaslight me into turning against them just because you're prejudiced."

"I have tried to be reasonable—"

Kaia interrupted. "There is no mistaking the bond-mate, Lyra. Whatever you believe, you clearly don't know the entire story."

"Or she's just lying and manipulating us like she has been from the start," Penelope spat.

Kaia shot her an almost pleading look. What was it for? Penelope narrowed her eyes. Was Kaia on the mermaid's side? *Or is she trying to play Lyra, to work within Lyra's penchant for games, so convince her to let me see Raven?*

Penelope had no reason to distrust Kaia. She closed her mouth and inhaled deeply, trying to calm herself.

"You can't just take away Penelope's ability to visit Raven without telling her first," Kaia said as she turned to Lyra. "The bond is powerful, and it's clear that you and the rest of the mermaids have something against Raven. So, it's not unreasonable for Penelope to be worried about Raven."

Lyra stared down at Penelope with narrowed eyes.

"We all are worried about Raven," Kaia continued, softening her tone. "They're our friend. And we need to know they're all right. Perhaps it will be best if you let Penelope stay with them all the time."

Penelope's gaze swung to Kaia. What was she saying—that Penelope should be locked up, too?

CHAPTER
FIFTEEN

"OR MAYBE RAVEN should stay with me in the quarters the mermaids have already given us," Penelope burst out, glaring at Kaia.

She couldn't believe that Kaia would suggest that it was at all reasonable for the mermaids to keep Raven locked up like they were doing. Had Lyra gotten to her? Had this meeting been Lyra telling Kaia things about gorgons and poisoning her against Raven?

Kaia sighed as she turned to Penelope. "We both know that will not happen, though. As much as I would love for Raven to stay with us."

"The gorgon's tampered with all your minds," Lyra declared, but she sounded more frustrated than anything. She was glaring at Kaia as she propped her hands on her hips. "Why, when I revealed to you the vulnerable state of my city—of the children—do you think to weaken me further?"

Kaia mirrored Lyra's stance and lifted her chin. "Tell me how I'm weakening you further by suggesting that Penelope will be better off staying with her mate? Tell me how giving us the assurance that you aren't mistreating our friend is something for you to protest?"

Penelope forced herself to relax, even though she didn't want to. Kaia had this in hand. She had to trust Kaia—and stop jumping to conclusions.

"I will not have the gorgon causing any further trouble!"

"What trouble has Raven caused?"

Lyra gestured to Penelope. "This! I should look at increasing our defenses, but—"

"Instead, you're arguing about a problem you caused by forbidding Penelope to be with her mate without warning," Kaia interrupted. "And you will not have this problem if Penelope and Raven live together here."

The guards were shifting from foot to foot, glancing at each other with incredulous expressions.

Penelope could feel the tension growing thicker in the air.

Kaia rubbed her hands over her face, sighing. "Lyra, please. Why don't you and I speak about this privately and allow Penelope and Raven to be together in the meantime? At the very least, it will prevent Penelope from causing more trouble."

"I'm not the one causing trouble," Penelope protested.

Kaia winced and shot her another pleading look.

Penelope folded her arms and looked away, again breathing deeply. *Stay calm. Kaia is trying her best, and Lyra doesn't like to be challenged. Let Kaia deal with the mermaid's ego.*

Difficult, but not impossible. As long as Penelope kept her gaze on Kaia rather than looking at Lyra's hateful face. Kaia was trying her best. She was trying to work the situation to ensure that Penelope could stay with Raven at all times, to keep them safe even with these mermaids who hated them.

Assumptions did no good, except for the assumption that Kaia was on their side like she always was.

Penelope wasn't used to the sort of situation where she had to sit and wait. She wasn't used to having to be sneaky. Even when faced with Finnegan in the past, it was always straightforward. Lyra was nothing like the dangers that Penelope had faced before.

For starters, she really didn't even know what Lyra was truly after.

"Fine," Lyra said eventually, waving a hand. The guards stepped aside, but Lyra pointed at Penelope. "But just know this. Any problems you cause will be answered on your mate's head."

Lyra viewed Penelope with a long, piercing look before she turned on her heel and swept off.

The same guard who had twisted Penelope's arms behind her now shoved her shoulder roughly. A twinge of pain shot through her, but Penelope didn't care so long as she could see Raven. The guards crowded in around her, trying to intimidate her, but she only walked faster, hoping to get there sooner.

They led her to a new location, not the simple but comfortable chambers where Raven had been previously. Instead, they worked their way higher and higher, until they came to a tall, spindly tower. Dirt caked the stairs, and Penelope was certain she saw rats scurry out of the way from the lightstone torches.

Finally, they reached the top of the tower, and a heavy wooden door was unlocked. Penelope was shoved in.

"Penelope?"

Penelope squinted in the darkness. The only light came from a distant glimmer outside the room. It appeared there was only one small window.

Something moved, and Penelope turned. Raven embraced her, and she hugged her mate tightly. She breathed in Raven's scent.

"When did they put you in here?" Penelope demanded. She was shaking again in horror at the situation Raven was in, as well as fury at Lyra for putting them in there.

"This morning," Raven replied. "But it's not as bad as the caves. At least I won't get rained on here."

Penelope's eyes adjusted to the dim light. A pile of straw sat in one corner and a bucket in another. That was it. That was all the mermaids had given Raven.

"I'm not letting you stay here," Penelope snarled. "If Lyra thinks I'm going to take this sitting down—"

"Pen." Raven put a hand over her mouth.

Penelope bit back on her angry oaths.

"Don't get so angry that you forget to think. We're all in a precarious position here," Raven warned. "And it could be worse."

It could be worse. Penelope bit back on several more things she'd like to say... mostly calling Lyra names that Penelope rarely used.

"I will not let them treat you like an animal... worse than an animal," Penelope said. "This is inhumane. I'm supposed to just ignore it? I thought Lyra might have killed you. If I don't get you out, she might just do that, anyway."

"But Lyra didn't kill me." Raven's voice trembled.

Not yet. But with the way Lyra was acting? Penelope didn't trust her. Not one bit.

Penelope hugged Raven tighter, not just because of the urge to protect her mate but also because of the fear that she wouldn't be able to. If Lyra did something unthinkable, how could Penelope stop her?

"Listen," Raven said, pitching their voice low and urgent, "I heard the guards talking earlier today, after they put me in here. I think Lyra and the rest of the mermaids blame me for the kraken attacks."

Penelope let out a huff. "That's ridiculous. Just because Lyra's village was attacked while we were there—"

"No." Raven pulled away from Penelope slightly. "You don't understand. The city is under attack. It's not just the village. It's this entire place. The attacks started last year. They think it started at the same I drank from the thunder springs."

Penelope's eyes searched over Raven's face veil. Even if it wasn't so dark in here, she wouldn't be able to see anything, but it was still a force of habit. "What do you mean?"

"I mean, the mermaids think I became a gorgon, and my mere existence caused the krakens to attack them," Raven said. "Their fear and hatred of gorgons run far deeper than we realize."

Penelope's heart pounded against her ribs as a bitter taste crept into her mouth. "No, that's impossible."

"What if it's not?" Raven asked, shoulders slumping.

"It is."

"Penelope, we know that magic is interconnected. What if there are ripples we can't see? I'm something new, or at least something that hasn't been seen in millennia. And if the krakens attacked at the same time—"

"Then it's a coincidence." Penelope caught both of Raven's hands in hers. They were ice cold. "It's not true. Lyra is a liar. We can't trust anything she or the mermaids say. How do we even know that the krakens are attacking? They're docile."

Raven sighed heavily. "I know."

"You can't. You only heard—"

"I *know*," Raven repeated.

Penelope fell silent, recognizing that tone. It was more than just taking the mermaids' word on the matter. Raven had prophetic abilities, and they must have used them somehow to confirm what they had overheard.

"My being a gorgon has a reach we don't understand," Raven continued softly.

"That doesn't mean you're responsible for what's happening here."

"Not intentionally. But intentions don't mean I'm not responsible."

Penelope closed her eyes. From the start of when she met Raven, they had been fighting with the idea that they were cursed, that this was a punishment. Penelope couldn't deny that being changed into something that couldn't even reveal their face felt like a punishment.

But nature didn't work in ways like that. Ripples in a pond after a rock was tossed in weren't a punishment to the water or the rock. Rains and droughts weren't punishments... they just were. Penelope had to believe that Raven's situation was the same. Not something that was done to punish them deliberately... it just was.

"Pen?" Raven touched her cheek. "I know you don't want to think it could be connected, but I'm sure it is. I just don't know how."

Penelope sighed as she opened her eyes again. "I refuse to believe that they are in danger just because you exist."

"Maybe it results from circumstances that were created before I drank from the springs... But mermaids know more about gorgons than we do. I'm not in any state to find out, but you are." Raven cupped her face in both of theirs. "I need you to get answers for me, Penelope. Find out what the mermaids know about gorgons."

Penelope was quiet as she turned this request over in her mind. Back on land, Lyra certainly wasn't interested in sharing any information about gorgons with them. Was it really something that would change now?

"I don't think Lyra is going to tell me anything," she said doubtfully. "She only puts up with me because I'm a dragon, and she wants us for something. Besides, I will not let you rot away here."

Raven lowered their hands. "Then talk to the others and get them to help. I'm sure Lyra will jump at the chance to talk about how wicked I am for being a gorgon."

Penelope flinched. Yes, that she would.

"But there may be ways to parse out the truth from it," Raven continued. "And as for this place... Well, it's not that bad. I have a self-cleaning chamber pot over there, and the straw is quite fresh and smells nice."

Penelope looked first at the bucket, then at the pile of straw doubtfully.

"It's kind of peaceful. Quiet," Raven said.

Penelope shook her head. "I still won't let you stay here. I'll get you out. I promise. No matter what."

Raven closed her hand on Penelope's. "Don't make that promise, Pen. Not when you don't know what the price will be."

CHAPTER
SIXTEEN

THE LIGHT STONES cast a warm glow over the small clearing in the gardens where Herja, Penelope, Kaia, and Wickham sat together. They hadn't meant to gather here, but they had found their way here individually. Now they sat in silence.

Herja wished for a sudden burst of creativity to get them out. Lyra's city was certainly a beautiful place, full of art and fine works... A beautiful prison.

It had been a week since they were brought to this mysterious place, and their anger had changed to resignation.

Lyra gave them everything they wanted, and so long as Kaia was there to reason with her, she even allowed Penelope to visit Raven regularly. Pen had taken to smuggling food to Raven, worried that Lyra wasn't feeding them, but her reports of Raven's demeanor seemed to be fairly accepting.

Raven had had no prophetic dreams, though, and Herja was certain that was a bad sign. Normally she would have thought the opposite, but this wasn't a normal situation.

"Does anyone have any guesses what Lyra actually wants with us?" Kaia asked as she kicked the water.

This little pond had none of the weird mermaid babies in them.

Herja was glad—she found it unnerving to look at the beautiful fish and know that they were actually babies. Then, babies weirded her out, if she was being honest. They were cute, yeah, but something about a tiny person who was incapable of rational thought just made her very uncomfortable.

Wickham frowned at Kaia. "What do you mean?"

"I mean, if she really was holding us in exchange for something from Eldavon, they would have at least sent someone to make sure we were all okay by this time," Kaia said. "I don't think she's holding us hostage. Not the way she claims, at least."

"Of course she's lying," Penelope snorted. "She wants nothing from the Crown. She's looking at manipulating us into doing whatever she wants. Just like she's been doing from the very start."

Herja flinched. Even though she agreed with Penelope, they couldn't assume that they were speaking in confidence. Who knew what magical eavesdropping Lyra had on them? She opened her mouth to point this out, but Kaia spoke over her.

"Excuse me for hoping that Lyra doesn't want to just have us kicking around waiting for the krakens to break in," she snapped. "But what does she want? I thought maybe she wanted us to help reinforce the shields. Then maybe to fight the krakens. But she's just keeping us on tenterhooks."

"Maybe so that once she asks us for whatever it is she wants, we'll give it to her because we're so eager to get home?" Wickham suggested.

"Wait," Herja said, lifting her hands. "We can't talk like this. Mermaids have magic we don't know about—she could be listening in on us, or there could be some invisible person hovering behind us taking notes about what we're talking about."

Her companions stared at her like she had grown a second head, but Herja only stared back at them. Lyra was too clever to let them figure out a way to escape without her knowing. And that meant listening to their conversations somehow.

Wickham ran his fingers through his hair. He wore it loose today. "So, what? We're supposed to just... not talk? At all?"

Penelope lay back on the grassy hill, her jaw clenched.

"I don't know," Herja sighed.

"I wish there were more we could do," Kaia sighed. "It feels as though Lyra is waiting for something. But I don't know what."

Herja also stretched out on the grass, resting her cheek on her arms. So far, Kaia was the only person in their little group who had done anything with Lyra unless Penelope insisted she see Raven.

Was that what Lyra was waiting for? She knew Kaia wasn't the 'leader' of the group. When they were in camp, it ended up being Penelope, Adina... and Herja herself. Moreso than any of the others, Penelope was the leader. But she also had that one logical moment in the vote where she asked for the others to stop treating her like the leader.

Mermaids, from what Herja had seen, had a stricter sense of hierarchy than Eldavon did...

"Kaia," Herja said, not moving, "I need you to do something for me."
"What?"

"Arrange for me to have a meeting with Lyra."

"Wh—Yes. I can do that."

Though her brow furrowed, she nodded once and rolled to her feet.

The confused, questioning looks from Wickham and Penelope bore into Herja's back, but she ignored them for now. Instead, she sorted out her own thoughts and what she would need to say to Lyra.

Penelope sniffed, and Herja lifted her head. To her shock, she saw Penelope wiping tears from her face. "I want to go home."

Wickham reached over to pat Penelope's back soothingly. "I know. We all do."

Herja rolled back to a sitting position. "I know it's a difficult situation we find ourselves in, but with any luck—"

"I don't want luck. I want knowledge," Penelope interrupted, wiping her face more furiously. "I want to know what these mermaids want with us. I want to know how to get home. I want..."

Herja scooted closer, twining her hands in her lap as Wickham continued to rub Penelope's back. She was used to her fiery-haired companion being sure and steadfast. Were these cracks she saw in Penelope because she was tired of the weight on her?

"If we could figure out where the mirror is, maybe we could activate it back to the Institute," Wickham said.

Herja frowned. That was powerful magic, more powerful than any of them had.

"Maybe," she said because she didn't want to discourage Wickham's thoughts. The only bad plan right now is to have no plan at all. "Do you think you and the other witches could start looking for it?"

Penelope shot her a watery look. "What happened to let's not talk about things too much because Lyra could spy on us?"

Herja lifted her hands and shrugged. "If she is spying on us, what can we do to stop her? The worst that can happen is that she's always one step ahead of us. But if we all just sit around feeling helpless, then we will become helpless. So..."

She trailed off.

"Best to do something and fail, then just give up," Penelope whispered.

Wickham nodded slowly. "I'll see if I can at least figure out a way for the mermaids to let us contact the Institute. I'm worried about Adina."

Herja nodded, biting her lips together as she looked away. Now that they knew the mermaids had brought them here on purpose, she wasn't entirely convinced that the attack on Adina had been a coincidence. Adina told Lyra that she, too, was a princess, and shortly afterward, she was attacked by an animal that they did not know was around?

It could be a coincidence... but Herja wasn't sure.

"Another thing we can do," she said in a low voice as an idea formed in her head, "is we can start trying to figure out how to do long-distance mind-to-mind communication. Or at least, maybe if we can boost Odele's energy, maybe she can contact Adina and explain what happened."

Penelope rolled to a sitting position, and Wickham straightened. A new, tense excitement pulsed in the air between the three of them. If they could reach out and contact someone on the outside, perhaps they'd find a way out of this...

Kaia reappeared, looking both hopeful and exhausted. "Lyra says that she will see you tonight if you will join her for a meal."

"I don't—" Herja started but swallowed back her protests.

They were in Lyra's power. And there were some things that she thought they needed to play to Lyra for. And so. She would play this game to the best of her abilities.

"I guess I'll see her during the meal, then." Herja tugged the ends of her short, black hair. "Pen, can you go see Raven? Work on your mind-to-mind communication with them. With them separated like this, we'll need to act fast if Lyra is unreasonable where they are concerned."

Penelope got to her feet. "And the rest of you?"

"I'll get the other witches, start looking for the mirror," Wickham said as he got to his feet.

Kaia's brows furrowed. "Mirror?"

"The portal out of here."

"Ah." Her expression cleared as she nodded, then turned to Herja. "What about you?"

Herja grinned humorlessly. "I'll start getting ready for dinner."

<hr />

WHEN HERJA WORE ALL-BLACK, it was just so she didn't have to figure out what she was going to wear day after day. Today, however, she chose each article of clothing with care. She wanted to exude confidence and power, the way King Lantos or Row did. Both wore all-black outfits as well.

Herja smiled to herself as she approached Lyra's chambers. It appeared she picked up on that without knowing.

She was welcomed into Lyra's chambers, which were so golden it hurt Herja's eyes. Everything shimmered and shone. Precious jewels lined the walls in mosaics, the smallest the size of Herja's head. Clearly, this place intimidated people with its opulence.

Lyra had likewise dressed to intimidate. A sleek, glittering gold dress that hugged her like a second skin with cropped-out sections that in Eldavon would have been indecent.

Herja ignored it. From her last conversation with Kaia, Lyra used revealing clothing to put off the students and make them feel uncertain and embarrassed. But Herja grew up sharing a room with others. It wasn't as though she'd never had someone accidentally barge in on her changing or vice versa.

"You look lovely, Herja," Lyra said as she gestured to a chair at the foot of the table. "Sit, eat."

Herja took her seat and gazed at the plethora of silverware on either side of her plate. The table was laden with lots of food, and a dozen servants stood on either side, ready to serve.

Yep. This whole situation was meant to intimidate her.

Herja sighed as she gathered all but one fork and one spoon and set it aside. "I do not know how to use all this, so if you want me to eat, I'll have to eat the way I know how. So. Another thing you need to know is that I don't get the subtle societal conventions that come easily to other people."

Lyra laughed musically. "I've noticed that about you."

"So." Herja waved off a servant who came to dish her up some food and instead loaded her plate. "What do you want from us, Lyra? When are you going to let us go home?"

Lyra lifted her eyebrows. "Are you not comfortable—"

"Nope."

Lyra seemed startled at Herja's interruption.

"We're not comfortable, and you know that." Herja deliberately rested her elbows on the table as she leaned forward. "You want something from us. So tell me what it is. I'll take it back to the others, and we can decide whether we do it for you or if we refuse. Trying to be all clever and manipulative is only wasting all our time."

Lyra leaned back in her chair, tapping her fingers against the table. She finally snorted and picked up her goblet. "You have no diplomatic skills."

"Never said I did."

"We mermaids have been gathering kraken ink for Eldavon for

decades. Now that Eldavon has been messing around with magic beyond them, the krakens have become aggressive toward us," Lyra stated.

"I'm willing to accept the premise that the aggression is because of your practice of gathering ink," Herja replied. "However, the moment you claim we're 'messing around' with magic just tells me you blame Raven for this. What reason could they have to make the krakens attack you?"

Lyra sipped her drink, eyes never leaving Herja. She emptied her goblet and held it out for a refill as she spoke. "You, children of Eldavon, owe the mermaids a debt. There is no leaving this city while the krakens are attacking."

"So you want us to... what? Drive them away?"

"Yes."

Herja narrowed her eyes at Lyra. "And afterward? You'll let us go, or you'll try to use us as your own little army against other mermaid and triton kingdoms?"

Lyra laughed. "Don't pretend that you know the game, little Herja. Drive back the krakens, and we will let you go."

"And Raven?"

"If you'll take them with you, then I have no desire to keep them in my walls."

Herja studied Lyra deeply, trying to figure out what she was thinking. "So when you kept being aggressive to Raven, you were hoping to send them back to the Institute, were you? So that you could keep us without getting them?"

Lyra laughed again. "Oh, dear Herja. No. No, the plan was originally only to have the gorgon. I'm convinced that they are the key to driving the kraken back."

Herja stiffened, frowning. "What do you mean?"

"I only changed my mind after Penelope declared Raven her mate. I couldn't just take them without consequences. And for that reason, I am giving you a chance to figure this out, Herja. Because I'm pretty sure your red-haired friend will get herself killed trying to stop my plan."

Herja's blood ran cold to her core. "What is your plan?"

Lyra shook her head and drank from her goblet again. "Pray you don't find out, Herja. Now leave."

Herja stood. As she headed back to the chambers where the rest of the students were waiting, she couldn't help but wonder if Lyra was lying or telling the truth. But in the end, did it matter?

They had to figure out a way to drive the krakens back. Raven's life depended on it.

CHAPTER
SEVENTEEN

KAIA, Nolen, and Odele sat at three points of a triangle, joined by holding hands. Since Herja had found out what the mermaids wanted from them, the students had been working tirelessly. If anyone was going to contact the outside world, it was Odele contacting her distant mate.

All attempts to boost Odele's energy had failed.

The frustration was wearing on Kaia. It had gotten to where she wasn't sure this was even a good idea. Maybe instead of trying to escape, they should focus all their energy on stopping the krakens.

Do you really believe that Lyra will release us if we can drive off the krakens? Nolen asked in her mind.

Speaking mind-to-mine was the only way they knew for certain that the mermaids wouldn't overhear. Kaia released both Nolen and Odele's hands, exhausted from their attempts at the day.

"I'm going to get some food cooking for supper," she said, rolling to her knees.

Odele gave her a pointed look; since the three of them had been connected, she had also heard Nolen's question. But it wasn't exactly as though the question was a necessary one. All of them felt the same.

Once the threat of the krakens was over, Lyra would find another reason to keep the students around. She lied about everything. Why would she tell the truth about this?

The only thing Kaia was certain of was that if they didn't save the city and then get out of here, Raven would pay the price.

"Maybe we should try something else," Odele said aloud. "Maybe—"

Every light in the room blinked off, plunging them into blackness.

Kaia's heart jumped to her throat and started pounding as she let out a startled scream. Her voice seemed to echo, but then she realized that there was a screeching noise coming from outside. Moans, groans, and a thunderous roar reverberated through the walls.

Something touched her, and she screamed again, only to realize it was Nolen. His arms wrapped around her and pulled her close.

The darkness and eerie groaning only lasted a few moments. The lights flickered back on, but the ground beneath Kaia's feet felt off-kilter. She was horrified to see that the frames on the walls were all crooked and the ceiling orbs were all leaning the same way.

The three students glanced at each other and hurried out of the room. They found several mermaids hurrying down the corridor.

"What happened?" Kaia demanded.

One of them slowed. "The krakens attacked the foundational support of the cities. We're going to slide into the trench unless they're reinforced."

That was enough for Kaia. She joined the mermaids, rushing toward the damaged parts of the city, with Nolen and Odele close behind her. Several large pillars in what seemed to be a ballroom were cracked. Mermaids were racing about to brace them.

Odele and Nolen transformed into dragons, holding the supports, and Kaia, Jalene, and Lena went into a tunnel created by the mermaids, leading to the waters outside. The darkness swirled beyond them, but Kaia was determined not to allow herself to fall into a panic.

It took them hours, but finally the damaged foundation was reinforced enough to hold the weight of the city. The students were escorted back to their chambers while the mermaids extended the boundaries of the shield to prevent such an attack.

"Pen?" Kaia asked.

Penelope looked up from where she sat, hunched over a plate of food that she wasn't eating.

"Can we talk privately?"

Penelope nodded and followed Kaia out into the corridor.

Once they were outside, Kaia reached for Penelope's hand. She didn't have the energy for mind-to-mind communication anymore, but she still wanted to comfort her friend.

"Are you okay?" Kaia asked.

Penelope shook her head. "I want to see Raven. I tried to go before the attack but..."

Kaia nodded, resolution making her throw back her shoulders. With this attack, it was even more imperative that Penelope could see Raven... to make sure Lyra wasn't doing anything to them in retaliation.

"Are you emotionally balanced enough to see Lyra? Do you need me to go see her myself?" Kaia asked.

Penelope passed a hand over her eyes and didn't answer. Instead, she started down the corridor, still gripping Kaia's hand tightly. Despite being the same age, Kaia couldn't help but feel motherly toward her friend right now.

Lyra was in her throne room, sitting on her throne when Kaia and Penelope entered. The mermaid queen didn't look at all surprised to see them. What surprised Kaia most was that Raven was already in the room.

Their wrists were chained together, and their clothes were dirty. But they stood in the middle of the room, tall and with no shaking that would show they were hurt.

Penelope let out a cry and raced forward, releasing Kaia's hand. She threw her arms around her mate and glared at Lyra.

"Don't look at me like that," Lyra said in a bored tone. "I brought them here for you. I knew you'd come barging in soon enough, and I didn't want to deal with fending off your accusations while we waited."

Kaia hurried over to her friends. She frowned toward the shackles on Raven's wrists. "Are you hurt?"

Raven shook their head.

"Now that you're here, I have a few things to say to you, however," Lyra said.

Kaia felt tension creeping into her spine but forced her expression to be neutral. "What is it? We're working as hard as we can."

"The krakens have been increasing their attacks by a great deal lately. Ever since I brought you back here, in fact," Lyra said.

"Maybe they're trying to rescue us," Penelope snarked.

Raven shook their head and put their hands on Penelope's shoulder. "Pen, please. Don't make her mad."

Lyra folded her arms. "I do not get angry so easily, gorgon."

"Yes, you do. That's why you won't abandon the city, even though it would be better for all your people. Because your last words to your mother—" Raven cut off as Lyra jumped to her feet, her face twisting in fury.

Kaia's breath caught in her throat, but Lyra rolled her shoulders and stepped down from her throne, saying nothing.

"They can't help what they see in their visions," Kaia said, quickly stepping in front of Raven. "But while we're all here, we know little about gorgons. I've asked you before, and you have continuously refused to say anything. So tell us now. What do mermaids know of the gorgons?"

"Ask them," Lyra said, jerking her chin toward Raven.

Raven lowered their hands. "I didn't even realize I was a gorgon until Penelope and the rest saved me in the Storm Mountains. I was a terribly sick child. Physically weak, and I grew weaker every year. I could do nothing more than sit by a window weaving by the end."

Lyra narrowed her eyes.

"But then the Odentian prince, Finnegan, found me and told me he had found a spring filled with magic. The Silver Springs had revealed me as human. But I wasn't happy with that fate. I wish I hadn't drunk from the stormy springs, but I did. And then this happened." Raven gestured at themself. "If there was any way to go back to what I was, I'd do it."

"Am I supposed to believe that?"

Raven was quiet.

"It's the truth," Penelope insisted. "Herja grew up with them at the orphanage. They—"

"Orphanage?" Lyra repeated.

Kaia's fingers caught in her curls as she sighed. "You know more about Raven than Raven does. We have read the old legends, but that's all they are to us. None of us thought gorgons even existed until this happened."

Lyra hummed and returned to her throne. "You, Kaia, I will believe."

Kaia bit back a sarcastic "Thanks" and only nodded.

Lyra stroked her fingers through her green-blue hair for a moment before she dropped her hands into her lap. "According to our lore, when dragons and witches were at war with one another, a band of the first ones fled to the sea to escape their violence."

Was this the mermaid origin story? Kaia leaned forward; her interest piqued despite herself.

"The sea granted them its safety. It gave my ancestors their fins and gills and welcomed us into its bounty. But there were dangers in the depths, just as there were dangers on the land," Lyra said, her eyes taking on a faraway look.

"The krakens?" Kaia guessed.

Lyra's gaze snapped to her, making her flinch. But the mermaid smiled. "Krakens, yes, and more. Leviathans that cannot be described. Monstrous sharks that could swallow even a dragon whole. Sea devils and lurking evils that we still do not dare name."

Penelope shivered, her expression hardening.

Was Lyra going to say that gorgons were among the dangers of the sea? But how would that even work, since Raven was once human?

"So the sea created protectors for the fish-folk who would one day become mermaids and tritons," Lyra continued, her gaze moving to Raven. "One in every generation, who could foresee the future to warn the people when to move, who could turn their enemies to stone and sink them to the bottom of the sea."

"Gorgons were made to protect mermaids?" Kaia asked.

Lyra's expression hardened, her gaze not leaving Raven. "They were."

"But?"

"But they took that power and corrupted it. They made deals with the devils of the deep and built more and more power to themselves, thinking they could become gods."

Raven shook their head. "That's not me. I don't want—"

"It doesn't matter. It's the magic itself that was corrupted. You carry in you all the evil of every gorgon who lived in days past. It was locked away, and you freed it."

Kaia gripped her hands together, her breathing uneven.

"Now, whenever a gorgon is born, their mere presence foretells doom and war. Because that is what their magic is."

"No," Penelope said.

Lyra didn't even look at her. "And so you see why my people are getting restless. Because we have the means to end the krakens' attacks. We just must seal away those powers again."

"Kill me, you mean," Raven whispered.

Lyra shook her head. "Not kill. I do not wish to cause war with Eldavon, though. And for that reason, I am giving you a chance. But you don't have long, Penelope, to save your mate. One week."

"That's not enough time," Kaia protested.

"One. Week. Now the gorgon will be returned to their tower." Lyra gestured to her guards and glared at Penelope. "You may never see your mate again unless you save this city."

CHAPTER
EIGHTEEN

WICKHAM BOUND the burn on Odele's arm, silent. While none of them had been particularly happy about the situation, the news that Kaia and Penelope had brought back from their latest meeting with Lyra made him sick to his stomach.

Kaia said that she had heard voices in the spring when they buried it. Could there be some truth to the power of the gorgons being locked away? Could their souls have been tied into the springs, and when Raven drank?

He refused to believe that the magic would make Raven evil, though. Evil was a choice, and it couldn't be forced onto a being.

Odele stirred as he finished bandaging her arm. "I wish I was with Adina. I hate it here. I want to go home."

Wickham nodded sadly. "I do, too. I'm tired of feeling like something terrible is about to happen, and I can do nothing to stop it."

"And she looked so afraid..." Odele shuddered and wiped her eyes. "I should have gone with her. I shouldn't have let her tell me to stay behind."

Wickham reached to put a bracing hand on her shoulder. "Adina is strong and stubborn. She was already stabilized when we sent her through. I'm sure she'll be fine."

"But you can't know," Odele said in a low voice.

"I can't. But I can have faith."

The door to the students' chambers banged open. Everyone jumped to their feet, tensing. Wickham lifted his hands, ready to call on his magic and fight, if need be, but it wasn't mermaids barging into their space to drag them away.

No, it was Xena and Jalene. Their faces were flushed with excitement as they danced on the spot.

"We did it!" Xena crowed, punching his fist into the air. "We've figured it out!"

Wickham couldn't help but catch their enthusiasm. He grinned, his whole body feeling lighter even though he didn't have a clue what they were talking about.

"Did what?" Odele demanded.

Jalene and Xena beamed at one another. "We figured out how to combine our magic and have fire underwater."

"Remember how the krakens ran when we shot fire at them?" Xena said, bouncing on his toes. "I can just bet that they'll scram once we're sending fireballs at the under the water. But we need you around, Wick, when we go out. Just in case something goes wrong."

"Go out?" Wickham imagined the pitch darkness that pressed against every window in the city.

One of the mermaids he'd managed to get to talk to him said that they were three kilometers deep, sitting on the edge of a trench that ran down another seven kilometers to thermal vents where the mermaids mined for their treasures.

"The weight of the water will crush you," he said, even as he followed them.

Jalene waved her hand impatiently. "If the weight of the ocean was to fall on us, yeah. But mermaids have magic that will form a bubble around us, giving us air and protecting us from the weight."

Wickham swallowed nervously as he trotted after them, the rest of the students chasing after as well. Herja and Penelope objected, yet Xena and Jalene had already told Lyra, and she was setting up for them to venture into the dark depths.

Herja slid her hand into Wickham's. *I don't like this,* she said to him.

I don't, either. When we get home, I'm going to push to have actual medical classes over the summer. I need more experience in a controlled setting.

Herja nodded slightly.

Everyone said he was too young and should focus on his schooling first before he started delving into the deeper workings of medical magic. But if he was constantly in these situations, being the only medic available to his classmates, he needed more information!

We'll make sure you get that together, Herja promised him. *For now, let's just make sure Jalene and Xena don't die.*

Wickham nodded grimly as he set the future problems aside. Jalene and Xena finally led them to a room where Lyra waited with a half-dozen mermaids, standing next to a huge double door that led outside. Wickham's stomach knotted at the dark expanse beyond the door.

Lyra shifted from foot to foot, her eyes bright.

"Wait," Wickham called as she opened her mouth. "What protection are there to make sure—"

"There are protections," Lyra said. "Jalene, Xena, are you ready?"

Wickham reached behind him, grabbing the hand of the nearest person. *We need Penelope to contact Raven about this before they go out!*

Jalene and Xena both stood tall before Lyra as the mermaid talked about what a brave deed they were doing. Her words washed over Wickham, but he didn't pay attention as the rest of the class grouped together, holding hands. Finally, Penelope's voice reached them.

Find Raven, Wickham told her. *If they can somehow see the future and check—*

But it was too late. Even as he felt Penelope reaching out, searching the city for Raven, Xena took his dragon form. Huge light stones flared to life just outside of the doors, revealing the monstrous tentacles shapes of krakens just beyond.

Penelope? Wickham heard Raven's voice.

Jalene mounted Xena, and the two of them surged out of the gates.

Wickham couldn't stop himself. He yelled out as he leaped forward, breaking the connection with the others. "You can't!" he shouted, even though in the water they couldn't hear him.

He whirled on Lyra. "If they die, it's your doing!"

Lyra gazed back at him with cold, glittering eyes. "No. If they die, it's your friend's fault. If there was no gorgon, there would be no threat."

Herja took his hand and pulled him back again. Her expression was grim and torn. He could sense the reluctant interest; she wanted it to work.

As they watched the shadow of Jalene and Xena move through the water, Wickham's stomach knotted. The chain of connection between them all was gone now, but he still felt the tension from his classmates.

If this works, she's going to want us all to do this, Herja thought.

Oh, as though he needed to be even more nervous! Wickham's heart slammed into his chest as he clasped her hand, as though if he let her go, Lyra would take her away.

If anything happened to Jalene and Xena, they wouldn't be able to get to them.

The shadowy krakens didn't seem to notice the two. Xena's emerald-green dragon form was swallowed up in the darkness as the krakens beat their long tentacles against the shields of the cities. Their enormous forms relentlessly battered against the shields, testing for any weak spot in the magic. He imagined what they would do if they got through, and a chill ran down his spine.

But then, as if in response to their desperate situation, the ocean erupted with flames, casting an eerie glow beneath the water's surface. The searing heat caused the surrounding waves to churn and boil. The krakens recoiled, their inhuman screams echoing through the water. The city shook beneath Wickham's feet, and even Lyra looked afraid.

"Come on, come on!" Lena breathed, her hands wrapped in fists.

Beside her, Victor stood right against the window, his face pressed into the glass. "I can't see them!"

The flames kept pouring out. Wickham traced them with his eyes until the bubbling, roaring ocean obscured even that. The massive light stones flicked, then blinked out.

Leaving everything beyond the windows black.

"Your Grace," one mermaid shouted. "Reports from all over the city —the krakens, they're..."

She held her hands to her temples, her eyes screwed shut.

Lyra turned, a desperate light in her eyes. "What is happening?"

The guard lifted her head. "The krakens are retreating. Their attacks have ceased."

Lyra let out a sound halfway between a cry of relief and a sob. She sagged against the guard as the other mermaids shouted in joy.

But Wickham felt no such relief. He rushed to the window, pressing both his hands to the cool glass as he searched the darkness. Xena and Jalene. Where were they? A bitter taste rose into his mouth. There was nothing. Even the erupting fires were gone.

They... they...

"Everyone, join hands!" Kaia shouted.

The mermaids jumped. They reacted seemingly without thought, reaching to join hands with the students. Wickham grabbed Lena's hand in one of his, Victor's in the other. Kaia's presence was powerful as she forged a connection between them all.

And then it was as though Wickham was outside the walls, feeling a frigid weight on him. Darkness pressed everywhere and he couldn't see the lights of the city.

"This way," Kaia said, her voice lit a space in the darkness. It was like the softest candle glow, but it showed him where to go.

No, not him. Xena and Jalene. She had reached through the crushing depths to connect to them!

"This way," he murmured, adding his voice, and the light grew stronger.

"We're here," Lena called.

The light grew brighter, and Wickham could feel his classmates turning in the water. They battled against the icy cold and crushing weight as they fought back into the city. Xena clawed back through the door and tumbled to the floor, taking his dragon form. Jalene fell beside him, and both panted for breath, soaked through.

Wickham immediately started with what he could do. The first thing was to make sure they didn't have broken bones or obvious injuries. Once that was established, he looked up at Lyra.

"We need to warm them up now."

Lyra snapped her fingers. Two guards swooped in and picked up the witch and dragon, despite their protests, and carried them to one of the nearby rooms. There, they were given warm blankets to wrap themselves in. Both Xena and Jalene shivered, but their eyes were bright, and they were fully aware.

"You have done a great service to my city," Lyra said, sounding genuine for the first time since Wickham had met her. "Tonight, you will be celebrated as the heroes you are!"

"Thank you," Xena said. "But really, we're just happy we can help. All we really want is to go home."

Lyra smiled. "I know you do. And thanks to your actions, you are closer to being able to do just that."

Several of the others burst into excited whispers. Wickham's heart rose, and he turned to Herja, ready to celebrate this good news. But the look on her face made him freeze.

Herja didn't believe it. She looked even more grim and serious than she had before. And she wasn't the only one. Kaia and Penelope did as well. Nolen stood close to Kaia, worry shining in his eyes.

Wickham's hopes plummeted faster than they had risen. What did they know he didn't?

CHAPTER
NINETEEN

ALL THE STUDENTS were given new clothing for the celebration. Herja tugged on the uncomfortable, frilly dress she had been put in. It was just the type of dress that Kaia adored and would have looked fantastic on her. Unfortunately, it wasn't the sort that Herja could stand to have on her body.

Except she had already decided not to cause any trouble tonight because she needed Lyra to be off her guard.

The party had been going on for a few hours now—had enough time passed?

Herja slipped closer to Kaia and hugged her, making a big show of it. "I'm so happy that Xena and Jalene could get those awful krakens to leave," she cried, then, under her breath, whispered, "I need you to distract Lyra when I'm gone."

"What?" Kaia hissed.

"Just do it," Herja said.

She released her friend and beamed at her. Kaia looked confused but did a good job masking it, smiling and nodding back to Herja. Herja continued talking with various mermaids about how excited she was to return home. They only smiled and nodded in return.

Not that Herja believed they would outright say that the students weren't going anymore. Oh, no. They would not risk their queen's wrath.

But when they were all linked, reaching out to show Jalene and Xena the way home, Herja had done little infiltrations herself. She had only caught glimpses of what was happening in Lyra's mind, but none of it was good.

Now, she needed to leave this 'party' without arousing suspicion. Kaia made her way to Lyra, who was drinking but never refilling her cup and seemed to enjoy herself but never looked away from the students.

It was almost as though she suspected something. It was even more important for the students to play their role as easily manipulated children who thought they were going home soon.

Herja came to Penelope and Wickham. Wickham was nibbling at a cookie while Penelope swayed on the spot, looking like she was trying to dance but obviously feeling wildly uncomfortable about it. Herja threw her arms around Penelope first.

"Today was an immense success, wasn't it?" she enthused, then whispered, "I need you to stay here for another few hours. Lyra keeps watching you. She thinks you're going to sneak off to free Raven."

Penelope made a choking noise but seemed to understand what Herja was doing. She replied, "It was. I'm glad, but I'll feel better once we know the krakens aren't coming back... once Raven and I can go home."

Kaia was talking to Lyra, but Lyra glanced at Penelope and Herja when Penelope said Raven's name.

Should have seen it before now, Herja thought, but didn't allow her anger at herself to show on her face.

Mermaids couldn't exactly talk to each other when they were in the way. They didn't have voices like whales. They navigated and communicated by talking. Mind-to-mind. Lyra was constantly tapped into the surrounding guards. She knew what was happening with the students constantly.

Herja hadn't realized it until she saw the guard talking to Lyra about the reports of the krakens ending their attacks.

"Wick, I'm feeling exhausted," Herja said as she turned to her mate. She gave him a big smile, then kissed his cheek. Stay here so Lyra doesn't get suspicious.

"You should head to bed," Wickham said. "You've been through a lot lately—you need your rest."

Suspicious of what?

Herja kissed him again and pantomimed a yawn of what I'm going to do next.

She said goodnight to the rest of the students and a few mermaids. However, she gave Lyra a distrustful look before she left. After all, Lyra knew Herja didn't trust her, and playing too innocent would be more suspicious.

She headed back toward the students' chambers and smiled to herself when the guards ignored her. Normally, at least one would follow her.

But her ruse worked, and when she came to her chambers, she walked right by and broke into a jog, heading toward the distant tower where Raven was being held.

They needed to sort this out. And to do that, she needed Raven's powers.

Herja's heart raced as she made her way through the labyrinthine corridors of the mermaid city. If Lyra found out she was doing this, she would be furious. But Penelope barely had any time with Raven and never without a guard outside their door.

They needed to speak frankly, and Herja was concerned that with their innate mind-to-mind abilities, the mermaids might even spy in on private conversations if they focused their minds sharp enough.

It was worth the risk of venturing into the forbidden territory of Raven's confinement.

But if they were going to get out of there, she needed Raven's future-seeing powers to unravel the truth and devise a plan to escape Lyra's clutches.

The distant tower loomed before her, its structure an imposing silhouette against the shimmering shield. She swallowed as she headed toward it. Since Xena and Jalene had driven off the krakens, the ever-present tremors that Herja had tuned out had disappeared. The strange pulses of power in the shield had ceased.

Only after the attack stopped did Herja realize how much it was taking out of the city.

She rounded a corner to the base of the tower and skidded to a stop. A mermaid guard, looking bored, leaned against the doorway to the tower. She straightened when she saw Herja and gripped her spear.

"Who are you?" the guard called.

Herja forced herself to remain calm as she strode forward. "My name is Herja. I'm supposed to see the gorgon."

The mermaid squinted her eyes. "Er... I didn't receive any orders."

Herja smiled at her, trying to appear calm and in charge. "We're here to help, though. Lyra did state we are supposed to have everything we ask for. It's not such a big ask, considering what we are going to do for you."

The guard blinked, then smiled and stepped aside. "Of course not. I look forward to following you and the other brave dragons to battle against our enemies."

Herja nearly faltered. Battle. So it was true. Lyra had more plans for them. But she kept her mask up and nodded once. "I look forward to leading you. Now I need to see the gorgon. Their prophecies are necessary for us to take the next step."

"Of course. This way," the mermaid said, bowing.

Herja entered the tower, a shiver running down her spine. It was time to figure out what was happening here once and for all.

<hr />

"WHY DO I get the feeling that you're after something?" Lyra asked Kaia. A smile played about her lips.

At one point, Kaia might have thought it was a playful smile, but now it seemed razor-sharp and dangerous.

"Hey, I'm the one that was trying her best to help you on land," Kaia said with a laugh. "I asked you about mermaids then, and I feel like I have learned nothing. So how about it? Do mermaids get married or not?"

Lyra's gaze scanned the group as though she was numbering each of the students. That keen, piercing look made Kaia's heart race. Even though Herja had made her exit obvious, like she wasn't trying to hide anything, Lyra was going to figure out something was wrong.

"Mermaids do marry," Lyra replied. "To each other, to tritons, to land-goers. We don't care who marries who so long as all parties involved are consenting and knowledgeable. We tend to remain in our maternal groups, though, even after marriage."

"Nolen and I plan to get married someday," Kaia said.

"Oh?" Lyra frowned at Penelope.

Kaia could see that she was losing her. In a desperate attempt, she blurted, "You're right. I am after something."

Lyra's eyes snapped back to her, and it seemed like disappointment crossed her face before she nodded. "As I suspected."

"I want to go home," Kaia said. She touched Lyra's wrist. "I miss my family. I miss my mother and father. They're going to be so worried about me. Even if it's too soon to leave because the krakens could attack again, can't we send messages back home?"

Lyra's expression softened, a rare moment of sympathy flickering in her eyes. "I understand, Kaia. If I could get even a moment with my mother again...."

A hint of wistfulness flashed across Lyra's features as if she, too, understood the pain of being separated from those she cherished. But she quickly regained her composure, her tone firm.

"I can't risk it. Not right now. Using the portal will cause the krakens to return."

"But—"

"I'm sorry." Lyra shook her head. "You and your classmates still have so much work to do here."

"Please."

Lyra shook her head again, then clapped her hands together. "I can't let you leave or risk contacting your family, but I know what I can give you to make you feel better and ease the burden of your separation."

Kaia stared at her uncertainly, unnerved by this sudden turnaround. Lyra grinned at her, the way she used to grin on land, and a sinking feeling hit her in the pit of her stomach. Why did she get the sense that something horrible was about to happen?

"You say that you and Nolen plan to marry, correct?" Lyra cooed girlishly.

Kaia nodded, pressing her lips together.

"Then that settles the matter. I will arrange the wedding for you." Lyra clasped her hands beneath her chin. "I will have a beautiful dress made for you and new chambers decorated for the happy couple."

Kaia choked on her own breath, staring in horror. A wedding? "But—"

"This way, you don't have to wait," Lyra said. "I know how important fated mates are to each other. Won't it be perfect, Kaia? You may not have your family, but you will start a new one."

"No! We're too young to get married. We don't want to have a wedding until we've graduated—"

Lyra shrugged. "Waiting is overrated."

"Lyra, please. This is completely inappropriate."

"Why were you asking about a wedding if you didn't want one?" Lyra demanded, her expression falling. "Are you refusing my gift, Kaia? I have tried so hard to make sure you and your classmates were comfortable here."

Kaia held up both her hands. "I am not ready to be married yet."

"Nonsense. You love him, right? What's there to wait for?"

Kaia's heart sank. She would not win this argument. And she knew what it meant, too. Lyra was distracting her again. She had an intention of ever letting them go back home.

CHAPTER
TWENTY

WICKHAM WEARILY MADE his way back to the students' chambers, feeling the weight of exhaustion settling upon him. The celebration, the constant tension, and the uncertainty of their situation had taken a toll on his spirit. Add to it that insane declaration that Lyra had made. He almost thought she had done it on purpose to end the party.

Nolen, Odele, Penelope, and Kaia all trailed after him as he entered the chambers. Every luxury looked more like shackles than he cared to think about.

"I feel like I could sleep for a week," he said as he slumped onto a nearby couch.

He rubbed his temples. The worry about Xena and Jalene had taken more out of him than he realized. His brief renewal of hope only made the resulting crash wipe him out even more.

"I can't believe everything that's been happening," Nolen said. "It feels like we've been through a lifetime of challenges in just four short years. It feels like every year we end up with something else."

Odele nodded as she stretched out on the floor. "Yeah. And now you're getting married. I suppose Lyra's going to pressure you to have kids before long."

Kaia groaned as she sank onto the couch beside Wickham. "I'm pretty sure she already started."

Wickham winced. What was wrong with Lyra? Seventeen was way too young to be thinking about children!

But then, Lyra wanted reasons to keep them here. She didn't care about their health, physical or mental. All she cared about was getting what she wanted from them. Which was... what?

The door opened, and Herja slipped in. Relief washed over her face when she saw them gathered, and in a few quick strides, she joined them.

"Herja, thank the sun you're here," Kaia cried out, jumping to her feet. "Lyra is going to force Nolen and me to have a massive wedding!"

Herja did a double take. "What?"

"She said it at the party. I started trying to convince her to let us contact our families, and in response, she said that she'd give us a wedding!" Kaia's hands clenched, and she shook. "I can't take this anymore. We have to get out of here!"

Herja nodded, her expression grim. "We do. It's more important we leave than you realize."

Penelope got to her feet; her silver eyes were wide with fear. "Raven?"

"They're all right, for now, at least," Herja said, but there was an odd sort of stiltedness to her voice that Wickham wasn't used to.

He stood, reaching for his mate.

Herja stepped back slightly, shaking her head. "I don't want to be touched right now."

Wickham nodded. Holding her would have been more for his comfort than hers, anyway.

"I reached Raven. They told me they've been having dreams, disturbing dreams of being embraced by cold, suffocating arms. At first, they didn't understand what it meant, but they overhead some guards talking...." Herja trailed off and shuddered.

Penelope leaned forward. "About what?"

Herja met her gaze. "It's clear that Lyra intends to throw Raven out of the city to the krakens. Even after Jalene and Xena's victory. It was always her plan, no matter what we did."

The air seemed to disappear around Wickham. He swayed and barely managed to sit again before his legs buckled. "But... why? We've been doing what she wants us to do. We..."

"She said she would not kill Raven, though," Kaia whispered.

Penelope turned and punched the couch was a cry of hatred. "We can't let this happen!"

Odele quickly held up her hands. "Maybe it's not the plan anymore. What if she thought she would have to because she didn't think we'd be able to chase off the krakens? Maybe since Xena and Jalene stopped the attack—"

Wickham shook his head, but it was Penelope's black glare at Odele that made the other dragon fall silent.

"What will we do?" Kaia asked, her voice thin. "We can't let Lyra do that. We can't. But I don't know what to do. I can't even see how we're going to protect ourselves, and she has used for us still."

Herja nodded. "The guard I talked to spoke about us leading them into battle. Lyra has use for us, all right. She plans to use us to invade other underwater kingdoms."

Wickham pressed his eyes shut, not wanting to hear it. But he believed every word. It made too much sense not to. Lyra would manipulate them all. He could see it all happening. She'd throw Raven out of the city to prove to them all that their lives and wishes were nothing.

Serve me and have comforts or defy me and die. He could almost hear her voice.

He buried his face in his hands. What were they going to do? *We need help.* But there was nowhere they could go. Nobody to call... they were in this on their own. Lyra knew exactly what she was doing.

And now they were at her mercy... what little of it there was.

PENELOPE'S HANDS flexed in and out of fists. She wanted to scream and yell and do more than just punch a couch. She hated everything that was happening. Penelope hated these violent feelings, but she hated Lyra even more.

This shouldn't be happening. Lyra shouldn't have been able to take them prisoner like this. She shouldn't have had the power to manipulate them.

Penelope wanted someone to blame, but she knew in her heart there was nobody she could blame. Who was supposed to see this happening? Ealdwulf and West? They were following a tradition of negotiations with the mermaids. How were they supposed to know that Lyra had become something like this?

No. The blame game would help none of them. Nor was this violent anger. Anger meant they made mistakes. Penelope breathed deeply. She had to be calm.

Wasn't that the lesson Row had taught her and Herja in the Silent Marshes? Violence begets violence. If they wanted out of this, they needed to think of a method besides trying to punch their way out of it, however tempting that might be now.

"We need to escape the city," Wickham said. He threw his shoulders back. "Lyra distracted us from our escape attempts by threatening Raven. We need to get back to that."

Nolen nodded his agreement. "The way I see it, we have two options. We either find a way to all link and get the mermaids in on it so we have enough power to boost Odele's mind-to-mind communication with Adina. Or we find that mirror again."

"Yes," Penelope agreed quietly. "Before we're trapped in an endless cycle of violence."

Kaia let out a shuddering breath. "An endless cycle of violence. Why does it feel like we're already there? Every year, something happens. Something that threatens our lives. When I became a witch, I thought I was going to learn how to serve the kingdom. Not face this constant..."

Nolen wrapped his arms around her.

Turning away, Penelope wished she had someone to wrap their arms around her, too.

"I hate feeling this way, but I almost wish the krakens would destroy this city," Kaia whispered, her face buried in Nolen's chest. "I think I would, except for the harm that would come to all the mermaids that Lyra commands. And the children."

Wickham hummed. "If we could figure out why Lyra is acting the way she is—"

"Or," Penelope interrupted, "we could just not care about what's going on in her crazy head. We could get Raven, find that mirror, and fight our way out if we have to."

Her hands clenched into fists again, the helplessness trapped in her chest turning to rage once more.

"That will not end the cycle of violence," Herja pointed out.

"Neither is letting Lyra throw Raven out to drown or be crushed to death in that ocean."

Odele shook her head. "I understand how you feel, Penelope. My inclination is to fight our way out, too. But unfortunately, we both know it's not possible. We're outnumbered, and mermaids have magic, too. Even in our dragon forms, we won't be able to do any good."

Penelope's fists eased.

"And if we go for the violence, it'll give Lyra the excuse she needs to throw Raven out," Wickham said. "While we're compliant—at least, seeming to be compliant—we have the chance to reason with her. She's too smart to force us into a corner just yet."

"We are forced into a corner, though," Penelope muttered.

"No, not yet," Herja said.

Penelope looked up at her, hopeful.

Herja was the one who had spoken to Raven, after all. Maybe she had a plan?

"First off, we will not get through to Adina, no matter how hard we try," she said, her shoulders straight. "The mermaids are casting a low-grade mental barrier around the city."

"But that's impossible," Odele protested.

Herja shook her head. "From what Kaia's told me about how the mothers and babies interact, I believe that they're born with the ability to communicate mind-to-mind. They can project more than we can. So we have to find the mirror."

Penelope nodded. Find the mirror. They could do that.

"In the meantime, we have to delay Lyra's plans. Kaia, this is going to have to be you," Herja said, turning to her. "I need you to think from Lyra's point of view. Look at Raven the way the mermaids do."

Penelope's jaw dropped.

"What?" Kaia gasped. "No way!"

"Let me explain," Herja spoke rapidly. "You're empathetic and able to see things from other points of view in ways the rest of us can't. We need that. We need to know exactly what Lyra sees as so threatening, so we can counter that threat."

"But Raven isn't a threat," Penelope growled.

Herja turned to her. "To Lyra, they are. This isn't about saying Lyra is right, Pen. It's about seeing things from her perspective, so we can fight that perspective."

Penelope's jaw worked. "But I still don't like it."

"I don't either. But here we come to the riskiest part of my plan," Herja said, her shoulders tensing. "We need to give Lyra more reason to hold us, to try to... inspire us."

Penelope glanced at the others and was glad she wasn't the only one that looked lost.

"It's going to be dangerous," Herja said grimly. "And it might backfire. But we have to do a jailbreak. Lyra must be reminded that Raven is more important to us than our lives."

CHAPTER
TWENTY-ONE

PENELOPE'S GAZE lingered on the distant tower where Raven was being held. Her muscles were tense as she waited for the signal. As her mind raced over the plan, doubts sank into the pit of her stomach. What if they were making a mistake here? What if everything went wrong, which caused Lyra to cast Raven out of the city?

The point was to make Lyra see that Raven was valuable to the other students. But what if Lyra decided that this meant that Raven was inciting violence?

It was almost enough for her to call off the plan entirely.

But even as her thoughts spiraled, Herja's voice echoed in Penelope's mind.

Now! Go free, Raven!

Determination surged through Penelope as she grit her teeth together. Free Raven. It was their only chance at this! She reached for her internal fires and slipped into her turquoise dragon form. A few shouts nearby came from the guards watching her, but she didn't care.

Penelope launched herself into the air, beating her wings powerfully. She rose smoothly over the tops of the buildings, heading for the top of the tower. She landed against the tower's wall, her claws digging quickly into the stone.

It took Penelope about two seconds to tear through the wall into the room where Raven was being held. She carefully collected the rocks in her mouth and pushed her head in to drop them not to harm anyone below.

Then she slowly released her dragon form, climbing into the small room as she shrank to her natural form.

"Penelope?" Raven asked, sounding bewildered. They stumbled forward to embrace her, but they turned their head toward the hole in the wall. "What are you doing?"

Penelope hugged her fated mate tightly. Regardless of the circumstances that brought them together, she had sworn to protect Raven and would keep that promise. She only wished she could as easily escape the city as she had broken into this space!

"It's the only plan we had," she explained quickly, taking Raven's hand toward the hole in the wall. "I'm not going to Lyra throw you out of the city to drown!"

"Penelope, you shouldn't have done this," Raven said, shaking their head now. "When I told Herja what I overheard, I forgot to tell her everything. Even the mermaids aren't certain if throwing me out will help."

Penelope turned to them. This didn't seem like something Raven would forget to mention.

Raven must have seen the doubt on her face because they continued. "Some of them seem to think that the way past gorgons were treated is why my powers are so dangerous. To protect me from them."

"Maybe... but we can't risk it," Penelope insisted. She crawled out of the hole, but Raven grabbed her arm.

"We can't get out that way," Raven said.

"We can. I'll climb down and shift back to my dragon form, and then you can use the spikes on my back to hold on to until we get into the air," Penelope explained. "I can fly to where the others are, and we'll all go through the mirror and back to the Institute."

Raven caught Penelope's face in their hands. "But that's not the plan, is it?"

Penelope hesitated. "Maybe it will work."

"Don't give me false hope. That's not what a mate does. So tell me, what is the plan?"

Penelope's shoulders slumped. "The plan is to show Lyra that she can't hurt you without the rest of us going after her. The plan is to show that even if she isolated you, we all still love you and will fight for you."

"So getting to the mirror is just a smoke screen because none of the witches know how to activate it, anyway?" Raven pressed.

"Yeah. And mermaids have strong mental communication. This entire city is filled with a low-lying cloud of mind-to-mind speak, so we couldn't have told you without Lyra knowing everything," Penelope said in a rush. The longer they stood there, the more suspicious Lyra would get.

Raven nodded once. "We still can't get out this way. You're too big in your dragon form to have your shoulders inside the room, and I don't think I can climb down to your spines vertically like this."

Penelope glanced down the long line of the tower. A fall from this height would kill Raven for sure, and she couldn't be certain she'd be able to catch them before they hit the ground. Her hands clenched into fists, relaxed, and clenched again. If they couldn't fly out of this, what would they do?

"Can you break down the door?" Raven asked.

Penelope turned to the heavy door. She didn't have the space to shift fully. Her mind raced as it came up with a plan. "Stay back," she warned Raven, gesturing them to a corner.

Raven retreated.

Gathering her might, Penelope slowly shifted. Her body wanted to snap to that of her dragon quickly. Keeping it from turning in the blink of an eye took almost all of her effort. She ground her teeth as flames bubbled up, her neck lengthening and her head changing shape.

When she was satisfied she had changed enough, she let out a narrow stream of flame, concentrating it on the hinges. The heat grew intense, and when she heard Raven whimper, she snapped back to her natural form.

The lingering scent of smoke and scorched metal made her choke, but when she rammed herself against the heavy door, the hinge popped free, and it sagged outward. Penelope let out a cry of triumph and rushed back to Raven, grabbing their hand. The two of them raced down the stairs. Raven's footsteps were faltering, but they didn't complain.

So far, no sign of any mermaids. Penelope's heart slammed into her chest as she and Raven hurried on. A desperate feeling rose in her throat, threatening to strangle off rational thought.

She knew they couldn't get out of the city like this.

But she prayed to the sun, moon, and stars that it would somehow work.

Somewhere in her mind, she wondered if this level of desperation was exactly what Lyra wanted from her and the other students. But they were too far in this to turn back now. She and Raven were approaching the final landing, and it wasn't like Lyra would forgive them for tearing apart her tower.

They reached the final landing, only to find their way blocked by the mermaid guards. Penelope skidded to a stop, putting herself between the guards and Raven. They were armed with wooden batons in their hands but daggers and other weapons on their belts.

One of them, a mermaid Penelope, knew as Adriana stepped forward. "Penelope, Raven. Please do not make us fight you. We have no desire to see harm come to you. This escape attempt is ill-conceived. Please come quietly."

"So my mate can continue being treated like an animal?" Penelope demanded. She rolled to the balls of her feet. "I don't trust Lyra to keep her word when she says Raven won't be harmed. We're getting out of here. That's all we want. Stand aside."

"No." Penelope inhaled deeply, preparing herself to change forms—

Raven gasped.

And then something heavy dropped on Penelope. Thick ropes wrapped around her, and she twisted, crying in shock. All her limbs seemed to grow numb at once, and though she fought and twisted, the ropes only tightened around her. They glowed softly, smelling of swamp water.

"What are you doing?" Penelope yelled.

She stopped fighting to take better stock of what was happening. She and Raven were twisted in a net, their backs pressed together. Though the weave of the net was loose, Penelope couldn't seem to free her arms to pull it off herself.

When she tried to call her dragon form forward, she couldn't do that, either.

"I tried to warn you," Adriana said grimly. She turned to the other guards. "Bring them. Lyra will deal with them personally."

<hr />

KAIA KEPT her expression smooth as Lyra ranted at her. She and the other witches were on their knees in the throne room, surrounded by heavily armed guards, as Lyra paced back and forth, screaming herself hoarse. The dragons had all been taken away, and Kaia couldn't connect mind-to-mind with any of them, not even Nolen.

"And after I promised you so much?" Lyra stopped her pacing to glare at Kaia. "I promised you a wedding unlike any you'd ever seen, and this is how you repay me? By throwing your support to the krakens?"

"What do you mean by that?" Kaia asked. Even though the students had long relied on her ability to connect with Lyra, she was finding it harder and harder to do.

"You're in league with them!" Lyra accused, pointing at her. "You want to see my city destroyed!"

Kaia lifted her chin and leveled her gaze. "We were protecting our friend. You know it. You're just angry that your plan to make us forget Raven exists didn't work."

"Raven is not your friend!" Lyra yelled at her, storming closer. "Raven is a gorgon!"

"Raven is a gorgon and our friend," Kaia replied.

"You do not know what you are speaking about!"

"No, *you* don't!"

136

Lyra narrowed her eyes and propped her hands on her hips, her lip curling back in disgust. "Careful, Kaia. I have been generous to you. I have given you and your classmates time to come to terms with your new reality—"

"You assume Raven is dangerous based on centuries-old stories," Kaia interrupted. "You're following a tradition that states you kill babies. How is that all right?"

"There hasn't been a gorgon born in—"

Kaia raised her voice. "How is that all right!?"

Lyra glared at her. "You need to forget about Raven."

Kaia shook her head, but Wickham answered, "We won't do that. We will fight as hard as we have to so you don't hurt them."

"We will," Lena agreed while Victor nodded beside her. "We care too much. I don't think you understand the connection that we all have."

Icarus took a deep breath. "Even if I hated Raven, I would fight for them. And I like them. They're kind and funny."

"You fear the gorgon," Lyra stated.

"That doesn't mean we don't like them," Jalene retorted.

Lyra's gaze skimmed over them as a look that might have been understanding came over her face. It was as though she finally understood that this wasn't just lip service. They actually cared about Raven. However, the understanding vanished as she looked at them, and her expression hardened.

"You pushed my patience too far. I have tried to be understanding with you, but no more. Since the dragons were the ones who caused me the most problems, they will all remain locked up," she said.

Wickham growled in his throat. "And what about Raven? If you hurt them—"

"The gorgon can stay with the dragons," Lyra snapped, waving a hand at him like she was trying to shoo away an annoying fly. "And when they show their true colors and turn all your mates into stone, don't say that I didn't warn you."

Kaia couldn't help but release a sigh of relief. She had feared that their actions would make it worse for Raven. Perhaps their plan had worked after all.

"And what about us?" Lena asked.

Lyra looked down her nose at the witches. "Yes, what about you? Well, it appears you are your friends' only hope. I will only release the dragons once you subjugate the krakens again."

"And what about after?" Wickham challenged. "Will you try to force us to march against the other mermaid cities?"

Lyra narrowed her eyes at him and said nothing.

Kaia, however, had picked up something else in Lyra's rage-filled rant. "What do you mean, subjugate them *again?*"

"Oh, don't start pulling at strings, Kaia. You won't like what you unravel," Lyra snapped at her, throwing herself into her throne chair. She glared at them for a long moment before shaking her head. "I had planned on letting you all contact your loved ones on the surface. I'd figured out how to boost your mental connections."

Wait, what? Even though Kaia knew she couldn't believe Lyra's words, her heart still jumped and crashed into her ribs.

Lyra smiled at them, undoubtedly seeing the hope in all their faces. "Now, however, I certainly can't trust you to do it. You could have let your families know you'll right. You could have learned if Adina was healing. Now... now that will not happen."'

"You're lying," Icarus said.

Lyra's gaze snapped to him.

"You never would have let us contact anyone on the surface because then they might figure out where you took us," Icarus continued, shaking. "And then they'd be able to get us back. You're only saying this because you want to hurt us."

"Be quiet."

Kaia bristled. "If you would stop being selfish for two minutes—"

Lyra leaped to her feet. "Selfish? Me? I'm doing what I have to do. Don't call me selfish. This city will be saved. Take them to their chambers," she snapped suddenly at the guard, still glaring at all of them. "I'm sick of their stupid faces."

CHAPTER
TWENTY-TWO

HERJA HELD her hands out to the teensy, tiny fire they had lit using some of the straw Lyra had given them for beds. Rather than the towers, they were now in the 'basement' area of the city, close to the edges, where it was cold and damp. And dark. They had a few light stones in the ceiling, but they were so small and provided next to no light.

Nolen paced back and forth in the small space, pumping his arms. Though he claimed it was so he could stay warm, the restless energy emanating from him was enough to set Heraj's teeth on edge.

"We should probably talk about it," Xena said suddenly. He sat between Penelope and Odele, with Raven on Penelope's other side, next to Herja.

"Talk about what?" Nolen asked tersely as he spun on his heel.

Xena rubbed the back of his neck. "Whether this was the right choice. Whether we made things safer for Raven or worse for all of us."

"I'm sure it was the right choice," Herja said, sitting up straighter. Since she was the one who pushed this the hardest, she felt obligated not to show her own nerves show.

She couldn't stop thinking about the witches and what Lyra might be doing.

By this time, all of them had tried to connect mind-to-mind with their mates, and they had tried combining their energies, and none of it had worked. Once, it almost seemed like Raven would get through to Kaia, but it was shut down hard.

Herja wasn't even sure how long they had been here. It seemed like a few hours, but they had been promised bathroom breaks every two hours and hadn't seen a soul so far. Of course, it wouldn't be the first time that Lyra had lied to them.

"If anyone thinks we should have done something else..." Herja started hesitantly.

"I'm not sure it'd be worth it to say if we did," Odele replied, her tone flat. "We all agreed on the plan. While we might be separated from the witches, we got Raven out of isolation. So, I'm counting that as a win."

Herja nodded her thanks.

"Maybe we could all take our dragon forms and fight our way out of here," Nolen suggested as he turned to the door. "We could melt off those bars and—"

Odele shook her head, and he stopped at once. "There isn't enough room. We'd be squished, and I'm pretty sure we're got nothing but ocean beyond that wall," she pointed to the wall opposite the door. "We'd drown ourselves."

"That doesn't mean we can't try to figure out a way to escape," Herja said as Nolen's frustration grew even clearer.

Telling him to calm down would only make things worse—Herja knew because she hated it when people told her to calm down. So, if she could deflect his energy and give it an outlet, it might help the situation.

She stood up and looked around the room, studying it.

It was cramped, just big enough for the seven of them to lie side-by-side, and when standing, she could touch the ceiling when she lifted her hands. So not great, but not the worse situation she'd been in. There was a pile of straw in one corner, but Lyra had also graciously provided very narrow bunk beds that could only sleep one person per cot at a time.

Again, it could be worse. They were supposed to be let out for the bathroom, and Herja guessed Lyra would still provide food and water. Though when that would happen was anyone's guess.

When she trialed over hands on the various walls, the one opposite the door was the coldest, and there seemed to be more moisture beaded between the bricks. So Odele must be right there, that the ocean was on the other side.

The tiny fire they had built was almost out, and Penelope carefully fed a few more twigs of straw into it.

The door was made of bars as thick as her thigh, bound by iron bands. There would be no breaking down that door. Herja ran her fingers through her short, black hair. They had to do something... but what?

Odele and Raven both left the fire and joined her.

"I keep hearing faint whispers from up the corridor," Odele murmured. "Guards are waiting around, and I just bet they're listening to everything we have to say."

Herja glanced around the room again, noticing this time that it had odd, darker spots among the bricks. She lifted a hand to Odele and then moved to the door and gestured for her to continue.

"From what I can tell, they have set the room up in such a way to help amplify our voices," Odele whispered.

Herja's heart sank. From where she was at the door, Odele's voice was as clear as though she were standing right there. That meant that the guards would hear everything they had to say, too. So that means they wouldn't so easily be able to come up with a plan to get out of here at all.

Lyra would hear about everything they tried to come up with.

"Then there's no point in whispering, is there?" Raven asked as they sat on the bottom bunk. "I guess I'm not surprised. Lyra would be foolish to put us all together with no way to keep us from causing more trouble."

"And Lyra might be a stuck-up, entitled princess, but she's not a fool," Odele said.

Herja shrugged as the rest of the dragons looked between them all.

She quickly explained what they had discovered, then moved to the pile of straw. She twisted small bundles of straw to make more compact, wood-like 'logs' that could burn a little slower.

"So I guess we can share all our information and figure out where we're at?" Odele said as she sat next to Raven. "Because I figure that there is something more to the mermaids' thinking Raven is behind the kraken attacks, besides them being a gorgon."

Herja nodded at her to continue as she handed a straw log to Penelope.

"I was thinking about the prophetic dreams you have," Odele said, turning to Raven. "But it doesn't make sense. How can you have a prophecy unless the future is already made? And yet we all have a million choices every day that we make, so how can it be?"

"Meaning what?" Raven asked, sounding wary.

Odele ran a hand through her pale hair. "Meaning, it has to be from somewhere else. My guess is that you have some sort of aural field that taps into the mind-to-mind communications that happen around you. That's why you kept dreaming of stormy seas on land. You were picking up something from the krakens."

Herja folded her arms. She supposed that made more sense than outright prophecy. "Then what you're suggesting is that when Raven had that dream about Finnegan's brother's death, it was because they picked up something from the mind-to-mind communication from the dragon and witch ambassadors to Odentia?"

"That is my theory," Odele nodded. "Or perhaps it's a combination of the two. Who knows, maybe the ghost of the old king visited them in their sleep."

Raven shuddered visibly. "Oh, I hope not. That's just too creepy. But what does this have to do with the mermaids thinking I'm the reason the krakens attacked?"

"Because I've been poking around. I think the mermaids have been using some sort of mind control on the krakens, using them to attack other cities and whatnot," Odele said, glancing at Nolen.

He nodded. "We've been looking into things on our own and

wanted to keep it a secret so that Lyra would have multiple threads to keep track of."

"But now that we're all here, there's not much point in keeping it hidden anymore," Odele said with a shrug.

Herja frowned. Though she understood where Odele was coming from, she would have liked to have this information earlier.

"My guess is that Raven becoming a gorgon had a sudden ripple effect on the over-linking mind-to-mind connectivity all over the known world," Odele continued. She nodded to herself like she had figured out all the problems she needed to address. "It broke whatever hold the mermaids had over the krakens."

"And so, the krakens attacked the city to prevent them from taking hold of them again," Xena finished. "That's brilliant."

Herja hummed, working on her third straw log now. "It makes sense if the attacks coincide with Raven becoming a gorgon."

Raven sighed. "But I don't feel like I have any particular skills in mind-to-mind communication."

"You also haven't had so much as basic training in it," Nolen pointed out.

Raven leaned back as though they were deeply considering this.

"The mermaids have been mistreating the krakens for decades," Penelope said. "Herja, you said that they're supposed to be docile, right? If I was a pacifist and forced by someone else to perpetuate violence, I'd turn to violent means of freeing myself."

Penelope bit her lip and looked away. No doubt she was thinking about all the times over these past few months when she got angry and threatened violence because of it.

"I think we all would," Xena said softly.

They all fell silent. Herja turned over these new theories in her mind. With the smallest pang of regret, she had to admit that it made more sense than prophecies. To think about all the moving parts and the sheer power the prophecy would entail. But it still wasn't as exciting as thinking Raven could see the future.

Still, Odele's thoughts on the entire issue were certainly understandable. And Eldavon didn't know what was happening because the vast majority of their information on krakens came to them from the mermaids.

Come to think of it, Eldavon only communicated with the mermaids. Not Lyra specifically, but certainly this kingdom. Why else would they not know about the strict gender binary they had between mermaids and tritons?

It unsettled Herja more than she cared to admit. Eldavon prided itself on its open-mindedness and equality. Yes, there were places where the kingdom needed to improve, but overall, Herja thought it was a good kingdom.

To be a party to such cruelty, even unknowingly, made her stomach churn. They had to figure out a way to resolve the conflict and make up for their part of this... if it wasn't too late. If the mermaids were willing to try.

Wickham reached mind-to-mind, but he was too tired to hold it for long. He'd unfortunately wiped himself out using so much magic lately that he knew there was no chance that he'd be able to reach Herja.

Nerves jangled through him, preventing him from resting, even though he was exhausted.

"I don't think we should do this," Kaia said from where she kneeled on the floor next to Lena.

The two of them faced Victor, who was likewise kneeling. His face was getting pale, but his expression was steadfast and determined. No wonder, considering he was a soldier. Wickham admired his fortitude while also wishing that he'd call it.

"I can keep going," Victor insisted.

"That doesn't mean we should," Kaia said.

Wickham glanced over to where the mermaid guard watched. On the latest attempt to communicate with Herja, he caught something that might have been from them. If he was right, Lyra would barge in soon, no doubt.

This spell that Lena and Kaia were attempting was one of the mermaids' spells. It enforced one's will on another, apparently something the mermaids had been using on the krakens for some time. Now, though, the krakens had shielded themselves. Lyra hoped that a witch's magic was different enough from a mermaid's breaking through that shield.

Wickham hated every part of this.

The door opened, and just as he had suspected, Lyra marched in. Her pretty face was twisted with anger, her eyes flashing. Wickham and the others got to their feet. He retreated to stand next to Kaia, his shoulders slumping.

No doubt they were about to get yelled at... again. He never thought that at seventeen, he'd be treated so much like a little kid in an abusive household. Doing as Lyra said wasn't good enough, no. They had to expect what she wanted and, more than that, had to accept that if she was angry, they'd pay the price.

Didn't matter if they had done something that made her mad or if she'd ripped her favorite dress. It was their fault.

"Have you made any progress?" she demanded, propping her hands on her hips.

"No," Wickham said. "And I'm sorry, we need to stop this. I can only imagine what damage it's doing to Victor's mind, let alone his body."

Lyra's scowl deepened as she narrowed her eyes at him. "You do not get to decide when enough is enough. Only I get to say when you stop."

"Unless we push too far and Victor dies," Wickham argued.

Victor stirred, reaching past Lena and Kaia to put his hand on Wickham's shoulder. "I'm all right. I can keep going."

"See?" Lyra said, gesturing to Victor. "He's all right; he can keep going."

"I don't care," Wickham said stubbornly. "Even putting aside his wellbeing, it's completely immoral—"

Lyra stormed forward, her fury erupting like a volcano. Wickham drew back, bracing himself for the storm that was about to break loose. He threw his shoulders back, determined that he would not shy back this time.

Her hand raised, and before he could react, she slapped him soundly across the cheek. The force of it sent him stumbling back. Kaia, Lena, and Victor all burst out with protests that were quickly silenced as the guards hurried forward.

Wickham pressed a hand to his face where his cheek stung.

"You insolent fool!" Lyra's voice pierced the air, dripping with venom. "How dare you speak against me? I won't tolerate your backtalk!"

Wickham stood silently. He refused to lower his gaze, though he knew Lyra wouldn't take kindly to it.

Lyra drew herself up; her hands clenched into fists as she glared at him. "I am tired of all of you trying to stab me in the back at every turn. That's it! No food for your friends tonight."

Shock rippled through Wickham's body. "What?"

"You heard me." Lyra smiled, her expression twisting in glee. "The dragons can starve."

Wickham's mouth dropped open, but even as he protested, the lights flickered. Erratic shadows danced on the walls. Then, all the lights blinked out at once.

Wickham's heart slammed into his ribs. This happened before the previous attack from the krakens.

A brief pressure probed against his mind, and then pain exploded through him. He screamed as he dropped, clutching his head in both hands. Images flashed through his mind, none of them making any sense. His lungs were on fire, his head splitting open, every muscle in his body tearing apart—

Then it was over. He lay in the darkness, panting; the pain went so abruptly and thoroughly; it was as though his body had not experienced it at all. If not for the pounding of his heart and his throat raw from screaming, he would have wondered if it was real.

Was this Lyra? Was this how she had decided to punish them?

Wickham had never experienced pain like that again, and he didn't want to go through it again. And worse... what if she forced him to watch the others go through it? He shuddered, rolling to his stomach. But if it was between the pain and possibly causing irreparable harm...

The lights came back on. Wickham looked up warily. Kaia, Lena, and Victor were all on the floor, their faces various shades of green.

The mermaids were clutching their heads, too. Even Lyra. A chill swept through Wickham—she hadn't caused it. So, what had?

CHAPTER
TWENTY-THREE

KAIA CLUTCHED AT HER STOMACH, sickness roiling through her following that terrible pain that ran through her. She glued her jaws together as she pressed her cheek against the cool floor. Everything seemed to sway back and forth.

A guard came stumbling into the room, panting. "Your Grace, there are dozens of krakens about the city. They're attacking the Mind Link."

Lyra stumbled to her feet, looking as sick as Kaia felt. Wickham, Lena, and Victor were all watching with confused gazes, and to Kaia's envy, they didn't seem to experience these after-effects.

Wickham kneeled beside her. "Here, take this," he offered.

Without even looking at it, Kaia took the thing he offered and put it in her mouth. It tasted sweet and minty, and after a few moments, the worst of her sickness passed. She remained lying on the floor, though, not wanting to risk that feeling coming back.

Lyra had been talking to the guard in a low voice and then whirled on the students. Her eyes flashed as her gaze raked over them. "Make the spell more powerful. Make this work!"

"Witch's magic doesn't work like that," Lena said desperately. "We aren't able to use other people's spells. If you'd just tell us what the endgame is—"

"The krakens need to be put under control again," Lyra hissed at her. "If we can't, then we're all going to die!"

Kaia pulled herself to her knees, leaning on Wickham for support. Part of her wondered why she, out of all of them, was most affected, but she pushed that aside. She saw an opening here, and she needed to take it.

Taking a deep breath, she got to her feet. Wickham still held her elbow, but she nodded at him, and he released her. She was still a little shaky, but she stepped forward, putting herself between Lyra and her classmates.

"We can't do what you want," she said, keeping her voice low so that Lyra wouldn't start screaming again. "But you already know that there's an option you can use. Jalene and Xena can teach the rest of us how to light a fire underwater. We can drive the krakens back again."

Lyra dug her hands into her hair, looking up at the ceiling. "Drive them off briefly, yes. But what about when they come back? You can't throw a little tape at a crack in the earth and call it fixed!"

Kaia shook her head. "No, you can't. But it will at least give us enough time for you to tell us exactly what is going on so that we can resolve the problem."

"I know how to fix this problem, and you're just not behaving!"

"Do you really know how to fix it?" Kaia challenged. "Or are you so caught up in your own head that you aren't able to see that what you think is the tape, and we're trying to build a bridge?"

Lyra looked hesitant. Kaia held her breath as she watched the mermaid queen's expression.

Yes, there was the possibility that they could all go out into the ocean. And using fire against the krakens would help. But that wasn't the main reason for Kaia's argument. She had to get the dragons out of their confinement first. She didn't know if her idea would work, but this was the first step.

"Let Wickham and me go with Herja and Nolen, at the very least," she said, clasping her hands together in a pleading gesture. She moved forward again as Lyra continued to look uncertain. "Please. We have a chance to drive them back, at least for a little while."

Lyra's gaze sharpened on her, her expression still faltering. "With the Mind Link down, I can't guarantee that we will contact you if you go out. You could be lost in the ocean and drown."

It was perhaps the first time she had shown any genuine concern for her prisoners.

A shiver ran down Kaia's spine. She imagined being lost in that icy darkness but bolstered herself. If her idea would work, then it didn't matter—they wouldn't be lost at all. They were three kilometers from the surface, and with magic spells over them to keep them alive, they just might have time to reach the surface.

And from there, return to the Institute and get real help.

"I understand the risks," Kaia said, throwing her shoulders back. "And I can't guarantee that the dragons will go for this plan, but it's worth a try, isn't it? If the krakens are attacking the city, none of us are safe. And I, for one, don't want to see the innocent people here killed."

Lyra's eyes flashed, and she drew herself up as though she took offense at this statement. Did she think Kaia subtly meant that she didn't care if Lyra herself ended up dead?

It didn't matter. There wasn't time to soothe Lyra's wounded ego, and she was already deflating. For the first time, Kaia thought the mermaid looked more than exhausted. She looked small and vulnerable.

"Right now, it's just about our only option," Kaia said, spreading her hands in front of herself.

Lyra rubbed her eyes as she shook her head, but she sighed, and her shoulders slumped forward. "Fine. Fine, you and Wickham can go to the dragons and try to convince them to help. But if they will not, then you will all be punished."

If that wouldn't be 'convincing,' then Kaia didn't know what was. She didn't want to know what plans Lyra had to punish them... she was getting so desperate she might do something unimaginable to get them to do as she wanted.

As the guards herded her and Wickham away, Kaia bolstered herself. This would work. It had to.

"I pray for your sakes; your dragons have learned not to be so stubborn," Lyra called after them. "Because if my city falls, we mermaids may escape—but you land goers? You will drown. I won't even try to save you."

⟨⊹⟩

WICKHAM CAUGHT Kaia's arm as she stumbled. She still seemed unsteady on her feet, and he didn't like it. While he was feeling as well as he ever had, Kaia was looking increasingly worn. Why? Was the attack on the Mind Link affecting her more strongly?

When they first learned mind-to-mind, Kaia and Nolen had taken to it as easily as talking to each other. Did this show that Kaia was more sensitive to mind-to-mind talk? Wickham had thought his own problems learning it was because of the roughness of his and Herja's relationship, but now he had to wonder.

He leaned into her ear as he steadied her. "What's your plan?"

He couldn't believe that she would really want to go out into the ocean with no guarantee of making it back.

"I'll tell you in a bit," she murmured back.

A shudder ran down his spine as he considered Lyra's parting words. All this time, he had assumed there was an acute danger to the mermaids. But now he realized he was viewing the danger to them as being the same as what he and his friends faced. But mermaids could breathe underwater. If the city did fall, then they could still escape the krakens.

He hated this. Hated everything about this situation. Now, more than ever, he wished he were back home with his parents and siblings. Rhett was in his first year at the Institute as a dragon. Tara was starting basics in school. Donnelly was going into advanced schooling, where he would soon start training for even higher education or a trade. His parents were well-established in their jobs, and everything was looking up for them...

He wanted to be around to see it through.

They were led deep into the city and finally came to an iron door. It was opened, and Kaia and Wickham were pushed into a dimly lit room. One guard hung a lantern on the inside of the door to give them more light.

"The queen will give you half an hour," she said, then slammed the door.

Herja jumped to her feet and raced to Wickham. She threw herself at him and Wickham braced himself for the impact. He wrapped his arms around her as she embraced him. They held each other tightly, and Wickham pressed his forehead to her head, breathing in her scent. She was all right. He could breathe again, knowing that Lyra hadn't harmed her or the others.

"What are you doing here?" she asked as she pulled back.

"Hold on," Kaia said as she pulled her wand from the pouch at her waist. She pointed it at the door. "Give us privacy."

Light glowed on the iron bars briefly, and Herja nodded her approval. Her hands still rested on Wickham's shoulders as she searched his gaze. "Well? What are you doing here?"

Kaia explained what had happened and what she had planned. "I figure that even if one of us can get to the surface, then it means Eldavon can intervene. We might get out of here."

"That might work," Herja said with a frown. "But the magic might also run out before we could get to the surface. Three kilometers going up... and we can't ascend too fast. Otherwise, it will rupture our blood vessels. I don't know."

"The krakens are intelligent," Odele said. "Maybe we can communicate with them? Maybe they would have a chance at reaching out to Eldavon?"

Wickham ran a hand through his long silver hair. "Whatever we do, we have to do something fast. If the city fails, we're the ones that will drown."

"And if that happens, but Lyra gets away, she'll blame the krakens for it all," Penelope said. She folded her arms over her chest, frowning heavily at a small dark circle on the floor that might have once been a fire. "And she'll end up getting Eldavon to use magic and force on the krakens because nobody knows that they're actually sentient."

The weight of the situation weighed even more heavily on Wickham's shoulders. Though he tried to keep himself upright and confident, he could feel himself bowing inward. How could they resolve this situation?

"Wickham," Raven said from where they sat on a pile of straw.

He turned toward them. "Yeah?"

"Put a sleeping spell on me. If I can have a dream, then maybe it'll be... well, maybe it will give us an idea of what we can do."

Wickham hesitated. They had less than half an hour now, and he wasn't sure exactly what Raven thought they could figure out. Yes, they had prophetic abilities, but it had never seemed to have worked on purpose.

Wickham nodded reluctantly. Even though he was still uncertain, the dragons and Raven had talked more about this. So, he went over to Raven as they stretched out on the straw and he rested his hand on her covered head.

The feel beneath the hood she wore was like a twisting mass of snakes. Warm and pulsing but rigid. It made him shiver in disgust despite himself. He would never get used to feeling this... whatever it was... instead of hair.

He pushed that aside, hoping Raven didn't notice. The last thing he wanted was to hurt them with his behavior.

He closed his eyes and felt the spell he wanted to place on them. *To sleep and to dream.* While Kaia was good at spoken magic, his specialty was in the magic that was just felt. Raven's breathing became deeper.

Herja wrapped her arm around his waist when he was done and led him to one of the narrow beds. All the magic he had already used today left him wiped out, and he lay down without thinking about it. Herja sat on the bed next to him.

"So, what are we going to do?" he asked, his eyes sliding shut as well.

"Wait," Herja murmured. "And pray that Raven wakes with a better plan than the ones we have."

CHAPTER
TWENTY-FOUR

WICKHAM FELL ASLEEP SHORTLY after he lay down, and Herja remained sitting next to him. She pulled the blanket up over him while Penelope covered Raven with their second blanket. Lyra truly was trying to make their existence here miserable... no doubt she thought she had more time to win them back to her side.

The half-hour went by so quickly, Herja almost believed that the guards had shaved some time off it. They marched in, their expressions grim and frustrated.

"Time for the witches to return to the queen," one guard said.

Herja got to her feet, shielding Wickham. Even though she knew that he and the other witches could look after themselves, she really didn't like being separated from them. These weren't normal circumstances, and Herja wanted to stay with her mate.

Not that Lyra would care about that... in fact, Herja bet these protective instincts were one reason Lyra had locked them away. Hoping to make the dragons mad enough to be reunited with their mates that they'd agree to anything.

"Wickham is sleeping," she said, keeping her voice quiet. "Please, can we have ten more minutes? You could stay here, too. And I know you can deliver updates directly to Lyra. We're still figuring out if it will work for us to use fire to drive off the krakens."

The guard narrowed her eyes. "What do you mean, if it will work?"

"I mean, this attack is on the Mind Link, right? And that's the field that hangs over the city, allowing you all to have such constant mind-to-mind connections?" Herja pressed, hoping that she could get some more insight into what was happening.

The guard nodded.

"They don't need to have physical contact, then. If we go out there, they might just retreat or swim around us but still maintain the mental attack," Herja said. "So maybe—"

Raven stirred.

Herja turned, her heart jumping to her throat. It had only been a few minutes—surely Raven couldn't have figured it out yet? Her friend sat up, stretched, and then slipped a hand into Penelope's.

"There's no use in arguing or trying to convince them to seek other means of resolving the issue," Raven said as they got to their feet, pulling Penelope to her feet. "Lyra has already decided. She's going to sacrifice me to the krakens in her last, desperate hope."

The guard let out a hiss between her teeth. "The queen wants to try the witches' idea."

Raven shook their head as everyone held their breath. "No. She doesn't. She doesn't think it will work and doesn't want them to kill themselves trying. She thinks I'm the cause and so believes this is the only way."

Herja reached for Raven, her heart in her throat. No! She wasn't going to just sit idly by while her friend was drowned!

"It's going to happen, anyway," Raven said, lifting a hand as though they knew what Herja was going to say. "Let's just get this over with."

Kaia scrambled to her feet. "There has to be another way."

Raven embraced her. "It's all right. I know what I must do."

Emotion welled through Herja. As much as she wanted to keep arguing, the words got caught in her throat. Raven just sounded so self-assured, so confident. It didn't make sense! Even if they had decided that this was what had to happen, why were they acting as though it was no big deal?

Penelope watched her mate with a numb expression. She shook her head, but no words came from her.

It wasn't fair. The mermaids had caused this mess, and now Lyra expected everyone else to fix it for her...

"Raven," Herja said, her voice rough with emotion.

Raven turned back to her.

"Is this prophecy? Or is it just a self-sacrificing streak?" Herja demanded.

Regardless of whether it was prophecy or just that Raven was tapping into the overall connections of the mind, she needed to know where this was coming from. If Raven was simply walking away because they thought it would be best for everyone. Herja wouldn't allow it.

For starters, Raven had done this before. Attempted to sacrifice themself when there were other, more logical options for them to take.

For seconds, it wouldn't change their circumstances at all. They'd still be caught here, with the krakens attacking, and no way out.

Because the issue wasn't the krakens, not really—it was Lyra. If she had any sense at all, the city would already have been evacuated. They would have taken refuge on the land and worked with Eldavon to build themselves a new home. Instead, she was counting on a dozen teenagers to fix her problems for her.

"It's what needs to happen," Raven said, pitching their voice lower. It was as though they were trying to tell Herja something...

But Herja didn't know what that was. She could only hope that this was Raven having knowledge of things that, because of the mermaids, they couldn't share.

Raven turned to Penelope again and hugged her tightly. Penelope buried her face into Raven's shoulder, and Herja turned away to give them privacy.

"I can't let you do this," Penelope said.

"I'm sorry, Pen. But this isn't your choice."

Herja flinched.

She was exhausted and out of ideas. As she woke Wickham, she couldn't help but feel like this was all somehow her fault. That, because she had taken on the mantle of leader in their camp, she should have seen this coming.

Her shoulders slumped as Raven headed out of the cell. The mermaid guards didn't stop them. The dragons all followed, with Kaia and Nolen holding hands. Last of all were Herja and Wickham. He reached for her hand, but she couldn't bring herself to be touched right now.

It felt like they were part of a funerary march. And she hated every step as they headed towards the throne room.

<hr />

PENELOPE STARED up at the massive gates that led to the dark beyond. They were the same gates that Jalene and Xena had had their monumental victory with... had that only been a few days ago? It seemed far, far longer. Her shoulders slumped forward as a feeling of hopelessness welled up in her.

She glanced to the side at Raven, wishing once more that she could see their face. Raven held themself so straight and tall, it was easy to think that they were confident that this would work.

Even the whispered plan to Penelope as they headed here, though, sounded so desperate. Raven might control their voice, but there was still an edge of fear in their voice when they spoke.

Lyra sighed as she gazed at the gathered students. She had allowed them all to be here, to say goodbye to Raven. Penelope found herself with very little empathy left for the mermaid queen. She itched to shove her through those gates, too.

Not that it would do much good. She'd just swim right back through.

"Despite everything," Lyra said, "I am not happy about this. I had hoped that it wouldn't come to this in the end."

"Don't patronize us," Raven snapped. "Just open the gates already."

Lyra peered at them for a moment before spinning. "Very well. Open the gates."

Penelope tensed. Her whole body coiled like she was a serpent ready to strike. She leaned forward slightly, ready. Though the others stirred around her, and Kaia sobbed openly, she ignored them all. Instead, her gaze was focused solely on Raven's figure.

The gates opened, revealing the inky darkness beyond. Penelope's heart raced.

"Raven," she called, unable to stop herself.

Raven stepped toward the gate. "It'll be all right, Pen. I promise."

They strode forward, shoulders back and head high. The hood and face veil they wore billowed around them as a cold front blasted off the black wall of water. They didn't even hesitate before they stepped through.

It was as though they had stepped into a voice. Instantly, the darkness closed in around them, swallowing them up.

The mermaids closed the gates, and Penelope threw herself forward, barreling toward the darkness to follow her mate. Several of the others cried out behind her.

"Pen, no!" Herja yelled. "You'll drown!"

Penelope ignored her. Ignored them all.

The mermaids tried to stop her, but she dodged them. She spun from their grasping hands, slipped through the gates, and was enveloped in the crushing cold. It shocked her, the weight, the icy water that stung her eyes and streamed into her mouth and nose.

She shifted to her dragon form, a burst of light emanating from the transformation. Her wings spread out to either side of her, stabilizing herself in the undercurrents that swept her away from the gates.

Where was Raven?

A ghostly glow came from the city, lighting up the surrounding water. She pumped her wings and legs, following the mate bond up over the massive towers. Finally, she found Raven spinning in the darkness as they were buffeted by the currents.

Penelope launched herself forward, fighting with all her strength to Raven. She caught up, catching Raven first in her claws, then wrapping her wings around them both. The strong flowing water pushed them higher, and when Penelope turned, intent on fighting her way back to the gates—

No!

They were shut tight. Even from this distance, she knew it. Lyra had closed the gates, sealing them out. Frustration welled in Penelope's heart, and she let the current take her away. She turned her attention to a window that they came up to as Raven squirmed in her grasp.

She smacked into the window and scrambled to find purchase, only to be ripped away again. She curled tighter around Raven, desperately hoping to protect them from the crushing weight of the water.

Only it didn't feel so crushing now. Was this what happened when you drowned? Did it feel like the water was getting thinner, like it wasn't so heavy? Her body wasn't so cold now, either. When she beat her wings, it was as easy as flying through the sky. Even when her lungs gave out, and the air burst from her in a series of bubbles, her inhalation felt like nothing.

It wasn't supposed to work like this. Penelope steadied herself in the current as Raven pulled themself free from her claws and climbed up her side.

What was happening? This didn't seem like drowning. She felt even more graceful in her dragon form than she had on land.

Sorry I didn't have enough time to explain. Penelope's voice came to her mind as Raven settled themself between the spines on her back. *This is what I saw. If gorgons were made from mermaids, it makes sense that I'd be built to survive beneath the water.*

But what about me? Penelope asked in shock as she found a rhythm in the currents. It was no more difficult to navigate than a strong wind above land.

I guess it's why you're the color of a clear lake on a summer day, all turquoise and beautiful, Raven replied. *You're a water dragon.*

As Raven said it, Penelope understood it to be true. It was the only reason she could survive like this. She was breathing as easily as she ever had. As she swept her wings through the water, she shot forward, easily coasting around the city.

Funny that I'm a water dragon when I lived my life in the Fire Watch.

From the outside, she could see how much damage the city had taken. The tower where Lyra had held Raven was utterly destroyed. Large portions of the city were flooded with water.

An image spread through her mind. It took her a moment to realize it was Raven, sending the feeling of what they were experiencing. Raven sat sitting on her back, hood down, and face veil was gone, the water having ripped it away. Their snake-like hair trailed behind them, breathing in the water eagerly. Feathery fans had blossomed, feeling as soft and fine as hair.

Not snakes at all. Gills.

Now, Raven said as the two turned together in the water. *Let's go find the krakens.*

CHAPTER

TWENTY-FIVE

KAIA BEAT her fists on the gate, pain spiking through her arms at every strike. Too much time had passed. She knew that. Her chest heaved with each ragged breath as tears streamed down her face. Images filled her mind of Penelope and Raven in the abyss, their eyes glazing over—

"No!" she screamed, grabbing one of the large handles. She yanked on it with all her strength, but it didn't move.

"Kaia, enough," Lyra shouted. "You'd only be killing yourself as well."

Kaia whirled. The guards had surrounded the others, their weapons ready. Kaia's gaze blurred. She couldn't focus on any of them. Only Lyra, standing apart from the others.

"Open it," she demanded. Her voice cracked with desperation, her throat raw from shouting. "Bring them back!"

Lyra's eyes blazed as she shook her head.

"BRING THEM BACK!"

"I wouldn't even if I could!" Lyra yelled. "Penelope made her choice! She didn't have to sacrifice herself, and she chose death!"

The words pierced through Kaia's heart like shards of ice. How could Lyra be so callous? She was entitled and self-centered, yes, but was she so cruel as not to care about the pain she had put them through?

Fury surged through Kaia, overpowering her grief. Her fingers curled into tight fists, trembling with a mix of adrenaline and rage.

"Penelope made a stupid choice," Lyra continued. "And her fate is on her own head, not mine!"

Kaia had never felt genuine hatred before. At that moment, she thought she knew what it felt like. It was an ugly thing that beat at her chest, tore at her ribs—and she embraced the feeling, letting it flood through her as she drew her wand and pointed it at Lyra.

Before she could curse the wicked mermaid, a guard swooped down on her. She cried out as the butt of the guard's spear smacked over her wrist, sending the wand flying. The guard's expression twisted in determination as she flicked the spear up, smashing it into Kaia's face.

The air burst from her lungs as she was thrown into the gates. Bone cracked, and everything went dark. Noise streamed into her ears like blood, and in the seconds it took for her to reorient herself, nothing made sense.

Then the darkness was gone. Nolen towered above her in his steel-gray dragon form, wings spread wide as he beat at the mermaids. Victor kneeled next to Kaia, pulling her to a sitting position. Blood streamed down her face and stained her shirt.

"Stay still," Victor warned.

Kaia shoved his hands away and tried to stand, but she couldn't quite figure out where her feet were supposed to go.

Nolen crouched, letting out a roar that reverberated through the room. Kaia clasped her hands to her ears as the noise seemed to knock about in her skull, making her vision seem to shake.

"Stand down," Lyra yelled at him, grabbing a spear herself.

Kaia's heart jumped to her throat. "No!"

Nolen let out a stream of flame, arcing it just over the mermaids' heads. They dove for the ground, several of the guards piling themselves over Lyra to protect her. The flame licked off the walls, the sudden thermal shock causing cracks to appear in the glass.

"Stop it," Lena cried from where she was still with the others. "Nolen, you're going to kill us all!"

But Nolen wasn't listening. Odele shifted to her dragon form, her eyes locked on her twin.

When suddenly, Herja was between Nolen and the mermaids. She stood with her hands lifted to him, her eyes flaring with a strange light. Kaia's breath caught in her lungs again as what seemed to be a pulse came off Herja.

Stand down.

The order was explicit.

Nolen hesitated.

Stand down now!

One mermaid lunged, driving a spear toward Nolen's side. Kaia launched herself forward, ignoring the fresh pain spearing through her. She grabbed the spear with both hands, letting her momentum throw it off course.

Then she collapsed and vomited.

"Enough!" Lyra shouted.

Kaia coughed, curling in on herself. Strong arms wrapped around her, and Nolen's worried face peered into hers. She clutched at his shirt as Wickham joined them at Kaia's other side.

"No more violence," Kaia whispered. Her head pounded, but that hatred she'd felt just moments ago was gone. She hurt too much to hate anyone. "Violence won't solve anything."

"Violence will solve nothing," Lyra said.

Repeating her or getting it through her own skull? Kaia didn't know—didn't care. She peered up to find Lyra was now standing between the students and her own guards, her hands stretched out just as Herja's had.

"Your Grace—"

"They will not hurt me. Even the dragon was shooting his fire above us. He was trying to make us stand down to protect his mate." Lyra's voice broke. Her shoulders slumped forward, and she hid her face in her hands.

Was she genuine? Or was this a trick?

"Xena, Odele, stop," Herja called.

Kaia glanced over to see the two dragons hauling on the gates, trying to open them. They turned with defiant, infuriated expressions.

"I know how you feel. I want to go out there and get them back, too," Herja said. She looked so strong as she stood there, her shoulders thrown back, her chin lifted. Grief was etched onto her face, but there was hope glowing in her eyes as well. "But Raven must have known what would happen. They didn't tell Penelope goodbye... they must have known...."

Odele gave one last half-hearted tug on the door. "So, Raven just led them both to death?"

Wickham placed both his hands on Kaia's face. A soft warmth emanated from them. Sharp pinpricks of pain washed over wherever he touched, but the screaming pain softened to a dull ache when he was done.

Kaia reached for Nolen's sleeve. "Don't do that again."

Nolen flinched. His eyes were wide, fear radiating in them—and Kaia understood. He was afraid of his own actions.

"I won't," he promised, bringing her hand to his lips.

Kaia closed her eyes. Wickham continued his silent spell until she knew he was exhausting himself too much. All the while, the others fell silent. The students eyed the mermaids warily while the mermaids gripped their weapons, ready to quell any threat to their queen.

Finally, Herja and Lyra faced each other once more. Both of them eyed the other warily as though they were afraid that one word from the other would cause a renewal of the violence.

"What happens now?" Herja demanded.

Lyra inhaled deeply, throwing her shoulders back. "With Raven's willing sacrifice, the krakens will cease their attacks. Once that has happened, then I can rebuild. You and your classmates will be useful in that regard. I'll trade you back to your kingdom for the supplies and workforce I need."

Kaia's heart sank. "That's the truth, huh? You were always planning on using us. But if you think that any of us will help you force the krakens into attacking other cities for you again—"

"Did I say anything about attacking other cities?" Lyra snapped at her.

"You didn't have to," Kaia snapped back.

Herja held a hand out to her, and Kaia fell silent.

"This isn't what I wanted," Lyra insisted. "I didn't want anyone to be hurt. Why else do you think I delayed as long as I did?"

Kaia closed her eyes—but as she did, something niggled at the back of her mind. Something that felt like...

She gasped and grabbed Nolen's and Wickham's hands. *Penelope!*

⁘

"REGARDLESS OF WHAT YOU WANTED, it's happened," Herja said, keeping her voice firm. Not angry. Even though her emotions roiled through her, anger would not help. Anger would only get more of them killed. "You cost two of our friends their lives and—"

She cut off as Nolen seized her hand. She reacted at once to pull away, but his grip was too powerful. Kaia's voice pressed against her mind, and she reluctantly opened it. Wickham joined with Odele's hands, and soon they were all linked.

I'm alive.

"Pen?" Herja blurted aloud, her eyes widening.

The mermaids glanced at each other. Lyra's hands clenched as she stared at the group. Her mouth moved silently, and Herja understood she could hear Penelope still.

We're both alive. Apparently, I'm a water dragon. Penelope's voice laughed in Herja's mind.

An ache of relief filled Herja's chest. She nearly fell to her knees as fresh emotion washed through her. Then a chill filled her. If Penelope hadn't contacted them when she had, how much worse could this situation have gotten?

Is Lyra there? Raven asked.

"Yes," Lyra said, her voice echoing in Herja's head at the same time.

An image unfurled in her mind. Penelope and Raven hovered in the water with the currents, making them drift softly from side to side. Penelope adjusted her wings to keep them in one spot while a massive kraken lingered before them.

They all gasped.

The kraken loomed in the water, four or maybe even five times as large as Penelope. Long tentacles latched onto the ocean floor, holding it into place as its eye, itself as big across as a dragon, was from nose to tail, lowered to peer at the two.

A glow seemed to come off the creature, its body undulating as it moved. Its eye was pure silver, just as a dragon's eye was. Wisdom shone from its gaze, and Herja got the feeling that, even as far away as she was, she was standing in the presence of something as ageless and powerful as the sea. She felt truly small and truly humbled.

I am Tidebreaker, the creature said. Its voice was as deep and fathomless as the sea. *Why have you wrought such violence on my people?*

"No!" Lyra cried out. She clasped both her hands to her head and the image ended. "No! I will not be subjected to this."

What's going on? Penelope demanded. *Can you still hear me?*

We can hear you, Herja said.

"Get your weapons," Lyra ordered, trembling. "We can't let this kraken continue. We must kill it—it's the reason for all this!"

Herja tensed. She quickly flipped from 'enough violence' to 'kill the beast'! "Lyra—"

"No!" Lyra yelled, her face turning red as she whirled on Herja. "No, I won't hear of it! We kill the creature! I should have known the gorgon would do even more against me!"

Herja pulled on Nolen's hand, pulling the group over to stand in front of the gates. She didn't release their hands, the connection pulsing powerfully through them. Her heart hammered, but she planted herself firmly in their path.

"You said that you didn't want it to happen this way," Herja said. "You have been acting on fear and prejudice, Lyra. Don't let yourself be blinded and make more mistakes that will hurt your people more deeply."

Tidebreaker doesn't want to destroy the city, Penelope said.

"The krakens don't want to destroy you—they just want to be free," Herja said.

Lyra's gaze skimmed over the students, her hands in fists. "Stand aside. I don't want to make this any more violent than it already is."

"Then don't," Herja said, meeting her eyes. "Stand down, Lyra. Listen to what Tidebreaker and the krakens want. Otherwise, violence is the only answer you will ever have."

CHAPTER
TWENTY-SIX

TIDEBREAKER'S massive body settled onto the ocean floor, creating a new current that wrapped around its ancient body. Penelope could feel the age emanating off the kraken, catching glimpses of thoughts from its memory.

Briefly, she wondered if 'it' was the proper way to refer to Tide-breaker, and what seemed to be a gentle chuckle filled her mind.

I am beyond what you can comprehend, little one: it, he, she, they, anything way you wish to think of me. I do not care.

One long tentacle glided through the water, offering a perch for Penelope to sit on. Raven clung to the spines along her back as she settled down. The skin was thick and rubbery beneath her feet, but she still worried she would hurt the kraken if she dug her claws in.

It moved its other tentacles around the two of them, forming a little box to block the currents just before its massive, wisdom-filled eye.

"There," it said, and though Penelope knew it was speaking through her mind, she felt as though they were above the water, talking as she usually would. "Are you comfortable?"

"Yes," she said. "Thank you."

Raven climbed off Penelope's back, holding themself down at her shoulder. "My name is Raven, and this is Penelope. You've been trying to reach me for some time, right?"

"I have," Tidebreaker said, its massive eye rolling toward them. "When I sensed a Grey One once again, I wept with joy. Your coming could not have come at a better time."

"I don't know about that," Raven replied doubtfully.

Tidebreaker chuckled. "No, you don't know. But I do."

"You called them a Grey One," Penelope said.

"It is what we call these like your mate, Penelope. But we don't have the time to discuss all of this; no doubt you have questions. No, our time is limited by the limited imagination of the one who calls herself queen...." Tidebreaker trailed off, grief and anger clear in its words.

Penelope reached out, making sure she was still connected to Herja. All her focus was concentrated on showing Herja what was happening here rather than trying to figure out what was happening— students and mermaids appeared to be in a standoff.

How long would it last?

"We are tired of the shackles of violence," Tidebreaker said. "We will no longer tolerate it. The children of land and sea have grown blind to what purpose the oceans have given them, and they have instead blinded themselves with evil. We cannot allow it to continue."

Penelope inhaled deeply, the water moving smoothly over her tongue, but somehow her lungs filled with air instead. "I'm sorry. Eldavon has been part of the violence against your people. We didn't know. But that doesn't change the pain that we have caused."

"I know. Your apology is well-accepted, but sorrow is not enough. This is but one city and others still try to enslave us to their violent wills."

Penelope lowered her head. What did Tidebreaker want from them? This seemed like too big of a problem for the students here... But she had to do something.

"What do you expect us to do?" Raven asked. "If you destroy this city, the others will only grow more violent."

"And if we do nothing, their violence will continue regardless," Tidebreaker argued. "I have lived a long life. If I had an answer, I would give it. But these little ones are only half the sea—we don't understand their land-minds."

"So you want us to give you options?" Penelope asked.

Tidebreaker lowered its eye. "Yes. Otherwise, violence is the only choice."

Penelope closed her eyes, trying to ask for Herja's help—but Herja was busy arguing with Lyra, trying to convince her to stop thinking of violence as the first option available to her.

This wasn't the only city. The krakens were going through a greater pain than she could comprehend. She herself had been more inclined toward violence lately, ever since the events with Finnegan last year. It wasn't just other people's inclinations that she had to find an answer to.

It was her own.

"We want to stop this violence," Raven said, sounding lost and bewildered. "But we don't know how. We're all so young. And I didn't want to be a gorgon. I wanted to be useful. Maybe I wanted to be magnificent. I don't know anymore."

"You cannot stop the violence. You can only give options," Tidebreaker said.

Penelope lifted her head again. "But you brought us here—"

"You came yourself. And you can give options to us, to the children of land and sea, to yourselves even. But you can only control your own actions. To do anything else would be violence in itself."

Penelope's mind churned. The krakens were attacking the city so they could free themselves. But the violence inflicted on them... what did the mermaids want? *Herja!*

A jolt, a pause. *Are you okay?*

Yes—ask Lyra why the mermaids started their mind control of the krakens.

Another pause. *She says that it's tradition to fight battles and claim territory without the violence that costs lives.*

So, they just outsourced that cost to others. Penelope's heart pounded as she passed this information to Raven.

"If the mermaids stop, will you?" Raven asked. "If they gave up their control, if they will negotiate reparations, would you stop your attacks on them?"

"Yes."

That was what they needed, then. The answers that might stop all of this once and for all. She relayed this information to Herja, praying that it would be enough.

If Lyra would stand down, be willing to show her vulnerability, and accept that she needed to do the work herself... then maybe they had a chance at this after all.

⁂

KAIA CLUTCHED HER WAND TIGHTLY, unsure if she should point it at Lyra as a threat, use it to seal the gates more firmly shut or put it away entirely. Everything that Penelope was showing them bombarded her mind so rapidly that she had a hard time keeping up.

Empathy, she thought. Herja had told her to think about the situation from Lyra's point of view so that she could figure out how to resolve this situation without making it worse...

So far, she had done little of that.

Her thoughts turned to Lyra's past, to the loss of her mother that had set this entire chain of events in motion. The pain of losing a loved one was something Kaia didn't know herself. With her sprawling family, she had lost no one close to her...

Except for King Diesel. He had been like a grandfather to her, and while she knew he passed peacefully, having lived a long, healthy life, it still hurt. How much worse would it be for her to suddenly lose her mother or father?

Images of their journey flickered in her mind. Finnegan in the Silent Marshes, the trouble with the Chameleon Sprites, Raven, and the second springs. This was yet another step in their quest to learn how to defend the kingdom... and the first time those convictions were genuinely tested.

All of them faced fear and pain this year. Anger. Desperation.

These were all things Lyra was feeling, and more than that. She had the fate of all her people weighing on her. She hadn't started on this, thinking she would destroy lives. She felt the sacrifices she was making would be worth it in the end.

With her grip on the wand loosening, Kaia looked at Lyra, truly seeing her for the first time. She saw the fear in her eyes, the weight of responsibility she carried, and the burden of her past.

"We have all gone to lengths we never would have before," she said, breaking through the silent standoff between Lyra and Herja.

Lyra's gaze flickered to her.

Kaia looked to her own mate. "We have lashed out in fear, in desperation. We've done things we didn't want to do."

Nolen's expression faltered. He lowered his forehead to hers as though he understood what she was doing.

"We have," he agreed.

Taking a step forward, Kaia lowered her wand, her voice filled with newfound empathy. "Lyra—"

"I don't want any of your pretty words," Lyra snapped at her. "You pretend to be on my side, you pretend to understand, but then you turn around and stab me in the back."

"We have not been honest with each other," Kaia agreed.

Lyra squinted.

"It started back to when you first came to camp, running from the krakens," Kaia continued. She shook her head as she remembered it. "I kept saying everything was all right because I didn't want to cause you more stress. But that was a lie, and I let my resentment toward you build."

"That is irrelevant—"

Kaia shook her head. "It's completely relevant. Because if I had been honest with you from that time, perhaps we would have been able to build a better, more open communication. Instead, I halted communication, and now look where we are."

Lyra seemed to falter. "I don't understand what you're getting at."

"I don't understand you. I don't understand why you thought this was your only course of action," Kaia said. She released Nolen's hand

and stowed her wand back into its pouch as she started forward slowly. "But I understand that you're afraid. You did everything you did because you felt you had no other choice."

Lyra shook her head. "I'm not afraid."

Kaia smiled softly at her. "You're terrified. And I know what terror feels like. But if I can extend compassion to a man who tried to kill me outright, why can't I give you compassion, too?"

"I don't want your compassion."

"You're trying to protect your city," Kaia continued as she stepped forward again. "You're trying to grieve your mother. You're trying to figure out what it means to rule."

Lyra covered her eyes with her hands.

"Think about the fear, the anger, the desperation you are feeling," Kaia said, finally reaching her. She took hold of Lyra's wrists and gently lowered her hands. "That's exactly what the krakens are feeling. They are terrified that you'll keep hurting them if they don't destroy this city."

"But we didn't—"

"You did. You forced violence on them. You took away their will." Kaia gripped Lyra's hands tightly. "They don't want this, either. They've just been pushed too far."

Lyra stared at her, and then she ripped her hands away. She snatched a spear from one guard and snarled. "And I'm still being pushed, Kaia! Stand aside. I have to kill the kraken and end this once and for all!"

CHAPTER
TWENTY-SEVEN

NOLEN GROWLED, but Wickham pulled him back. Kaia was right. They were caught in a cycle of violence here, whether they wanted to be or not.

Maybe Kaia could still get through to her, however.

"We will not step aside. We can get through this. That won't end up with more deaths," Kaia insisted.

His hopes were dashed like glass on a rock as Lyra pressed the butt of the spear to her chest and pushed her back a step.

"I have said it before; I don't want to hurt you," Lyra said, her voice brimming with a hardening resolve. Her anger and desperation over-shadowed any glimmer of understanding. "But I will. Your lives mean nothing to me compared to my city."

Wickham strode forward. He put himself between Lyra and Kaia, knowing that despite all of Kaia's attempts, Lyra no longer listening to her. Maybe they didn't have a chance at this at all. Maybe Lyra would attack Tidebreaker, regardless.

He knew in his gut that it wasn't the krakens who would suffer for it. Somehow, he knew the krakens would do their best to keep the witches and dragons from being harmed. Their quarrel was with the mermaids.

"You can't save your people with more violence, Lyra," Wickham said. "You were the ones who started this cycle. The krakens are defending themselves. They're offering you a chance right now to make up for that. They are offering you mercy."

"They're offering a trick," Lyra hissed.

Wickham shook his head. "You're forgetting something very important here."

Lyra narrowed her eyes at him. "What do you mean?"

"We're not you. The krakens are not you. You assume it's all lies and tricks because that's all you've known. You have the chance to save your people. But if you attack us and go after Tidebreaker and the krakens... you'll lose."

Lyra ran her tongue over her teeth, staring at him uncertainly. "I... I have to protect my people."

"Then protect them." Wickham held out his hands. "Give me the spear, put down your weapons, and protect your people, Lyra. Protect them against your own pride."

<hr>

HOW MUCH TIME do we have to get her to agree? Herja asked Penelope. She had released the hands of her classmates, but their mind-to-mind communication remained strong.

I don't know. Tidebreaker won't say. I think it's waiting to see if we can get through to Lyra.

Herja hesitated, her mind running over the possibilities. She realized Lyra didn't like her, so would her interference help or hinder any further communication? Lyra was staring at Wickham with a hard, blank face, and Herja couldn't wait to see if this meant she was considering attacking him.

"I have a question for you," she said, joining her mate.

Lyra's gaze snapped to her. "What?"

"When we were on land, and you kept saying that you didn't know how to contribute to the camp. Was that because you're lazy or were pushing us to be in the position you wanted us to be in?"

Lyra's lips pulled back. "How dare you?"

"It wasn't the case. You knew how to take care of yourself just fine," Herja pointed out. "So what was it? Or... was it something else entirely? Were you so frozen by your grief, pain, and fear that you couldn't find the strength to make yourself contribute?"

"Why do you all think that I'm... I'm..." Lyra swallowed hard.

"You are clever, Lyra." Herja smiled at her and raised her hands, not knowing what else to do. "But you're still a person. You have emotions. Penelope and I got a taste of what it's like to have everyone look to us for answers. That's you for your people. So be clever again, Lyra."

Lyra shook her head. "You're just trying to confuse me. I know what I have to do. I know what my mother would have done and what any other queen or king among mermaids and tritons would do. Even if I drive off the krakens, I must deal with them. They'll take everything from us."

"Not if you can negotiate a peace agreement with the krakens. You can find other ways for your symbolic wars," Herja said, lowering her voice. "You have already changed it, so the krakens fought instead of your people. So, find a new way."

"They'll think I'm weak."

"Let them. There's nothing weak about standing against impossible odds and refusing to take up violence."

⁂

"SHE'S RIGHT," Kaia murmured.

She inhaled deeply, steadying herself. She had already been threatened with that spear, but at least not by the stabbing end. Maybe there was a chance at this still. She had to take the risk because otherwise, they might as well go through the city destroying things themselves.

She held out her hands toward Lyra. "Give me the spear."

Lyra clutched it tighter, glaring at her. But she seemed almost like a trapped animal rather than a queen surrounded by her guard.

Kaia stepped forward again and gently wrapped her hands around the staff of the spear. Lyra made a strangled noise but didn't fight Kaia for it.

It was going to work. Kaia lowered the spear to the floor, bowing toward Lyra. When the spear was on the ground, she remained bowing as a sign of gratitude to the mermaid queen. "Thank you."

Lyra didn't reply.

"Eldavon has many proud traditions, too," Kaia said as she straightened. "And at one time, those traditions all served the kingdom. But time changes society, the people, everything. When a tradition no longer serves us, we must let it go. This tradition you have with the krakens no longer serves your people."

"And what am I supposed to do?" Lyra asked, her shoulders slumping. "How can I expect mercy from them when I think of everything that we, as a people, have put them through? What I've personally done?"

"You acknowledge your mistakes. You ask forgiveness." Kaia embraced her, pulling her tightly into her arms. "And you work to better yourself without the expectation of forgiveness."

Lyra lowered her head to Kaia's shoulder. "But without forgiveness, they'll keep attacking."

"No. They can leave without forgiving you. The only thing you can do now is to go to Tidebreaker and talk."

<hr />

PENELOPE'S HEART raced as communication with her classmates in the city fizzled to a stop. They were all putting so much thought and effort into convincing Lyra not to attack that they had forgotten to keep her updated. Now Raven's gaze was on her while Tidebreaker's massive form kept still.

A creature as ancient as Tidebreaker must have patience. But how much? What would it do if it lost that patience? How long did Lyra have to make this decision?

"Your friends are attempting to reach to mermaid's heart," Tidebreaker said, breaking the silence.

Penelope nodded, flexing her wings as she did so. The water in the tiny space they were in was warming, making her feel almost claustrophobic. Odd, since she had never been nervous in small spaces.

She wished she could be part of the conversation. But with the tension that had always been between her and Lyra, she doubted that anything she had to say would be taken well, anyway.

Sounds rippled through the water. Rumblings and the sound of distant echoes made Penelope shudder. It occurred to her that the currents they had been caught up in and these noises weren't natural. It was because the krakens continued to monitor the city, passing over it regularly.

Time seemed to stretch, but a fresh voice entered her mind just as she was reaching out again to demand an update.

Penelope?

It was Lyra. She sounded different from usual, however. Subdued, maybe. Her heart pounded even harder. It must be a good sign that Lyra was contacting her, right?

I'm here.

I... I want to speak with Tidebreaker. I want to end this cycle of violence. Please ask if I can approach.

Penelope lifted her head again. Hope swept through her. After everything they had been through, now there was a possibility that it would end...

"I heard her request," the ancient kraken said. "She may approach."

NERVES JANGLED through Wickham's stomach as he and the others watched the guards pull open the gates. Many of them looked angry, a few uncertain; there was even one that was sobbing aloud. They clearly thought their queen was going to her death.

Wickham prayed they had done the right thing here.

The ocean had never seemed too dark. Lyra stared at the rippling waves, closed her eyes, and stepped through. The guards watched, then quickly formed a circle, their heads bent together. They began chanting together—a prayer, begging the sea for their queen's safety.

Herja slipped her hand into his and gave him a strained smile. "Now, all we have to do is wait."

Jalene was leaning into Xena's side, Kaia and Nolen held each other, and Lena and Victor held hands and stared at the doors with intense fear. Odele was alone, and Wickham felt a pang for her. They still knew nothing about Adina's situation.

After several tense moments, one mermaid lifted her head. She left the circle of praying guards and approached them.

"Adriana," Herja greeted her with a nod.

"Herja. Are the krakens brilliant creatures?" Adrianna's silver-blue eyes searched Herja's face.

Herja nodded.

"They're intelligent and peaceful," Wickham added. "They only started this attack because they are tired of being used to fight your wars."

Adrianna lowered her head. "I didn't know. I thought they were dumb beasts. I was always taught they were dumb beasts."

The regret was written clearly on her face.

He wasn't sure how long it was before Lyra slipped back through the gates. Her shoulders were slumped, but when she smiled, it was as though she was a whole new person. Wickham had never seen her look so genuine before.

Penelope came after her in dragon form, with Raven—hooded and veiled once more—on her back. Penelope shook the water from her scales as Raven slid down her side, hands stretched out in front of them. Floating in between their hands was a ball of dark liquid. It glimmered and shone under the lights, changing colors as Wickham watched.

"We have made the first steps to peace," Lyra declared. "The krakens and mermaids will talk... and hopefully find a resolution."

"What's that?" Lena asked, nodding to the ball that Raven held.

Penelope, retaking her natural form, grinned. "Kraken's ink. Tide-breaker gave it to us in thanks. It looks like we've been successful... we have what we wanted."

CHAPTER
TWENTY-EIGHT

AFTER TWO DAYS of intensive talks, during which the students were once more given free rein of the city, Lyra brought them all to where the portal mirror was. Wickham had to admit he got a little choked up seeing it. After all this time, they could finally go home.

Lyra stood next to the mirror, her hands clasped before herself. She looked far more relaxed than ever, and there seemed to be a measure of peace in her that hadn't been there before.

"Before I activate the portal and send you home, I just wanted to say I'm sorry," Lyra said, her voice high and clear. "As I'm sure you are all aware by now, I caused the upset in the portal that brought you here. I'm deeply ashamed of my actions... but I am also very grateful to you for helping me see where I went wrong."

Wickham nodded, fighting the urge to tap his foot impatiently. He could almost smell the air at the Institute. It would be crisp, smelling of fresh air and snow. As soon as he was back, he would send a letter to his family to make sure they were all right.

A smile crossed his face as he imagined being greeted by Rhett at the Institute. He wanted to see his family so badly and was glad he could at least see one of his brothers sooner rather than later.

Lyra turned to Raven, bowing her head. "I wanted to offer an apology to you specifically. I let my ignorance blind me. I'm sorry for how I behaved toward you."

Raven nodded to Lyra. The mermaids had given them a new face veil embroidered with patterns of waves at the bottom and starry skies at the top. "And for me, I will forgive your ignorance. But I'm not forgiving your cruelty."

"I... I understand," Lyra said humbly.

She turned to the obsidian mirror and passed her hands in front of it. The darkness rippled, and the image of the Institute came into place. With its rising spires, the castle was settled in a light snowfall.

Wickham leaned forward, his heart aching to go through. But the students had already discussed how this was going to go. They didn't want to risk another trick.

Raven and Kaia went through it together. Then, once they were on the other side, they reconnected to Nolen and Penelope mind-to-mind to confirm that they were all right and that Lyra had sent them to where she said she would send them.

"All right. Lena, Victor?" Penelope turned.

The two rushed forward and entered the mirror, joining Kaia and Raven. Wickham stood next to the mirror as he, Penelope, and Herja ensured everyone went through. Everyone was quick about it, eager to leave this underwater city.

Wickham turned to Lyra, studying her. "Thank you for letting us go. I'm sure Eldavon will contact you to decide how to move forward after this."

Lyra dipped her head, looking abashed. "I'm sure they will."

Everyone else was through, so he took Herja's hand and stepped through. Unlike the previous portal, this one was smooth, as easy as stepping from one room to the next. The cold air slapped him, and he sucked it in, welcoming the sting of winter.

Penelope stepped through the portal behind him and Herja, and the mirror again went black.

They were back. A grin burst over Wickham's face as he let out a laugh. They were back!

"Wick!" shouted Rhett.

He turned his head to see his brother barreling toward him. Rhett smacked into him so hard it drove the breath from him. He hugged Rhett back as Rhett buried his face into Wickham's chest, sobbing.

All around him, there were reunions taking place. Wickham hadn't even realized that Lyra had contacted the Institute to tell them that the students were coming back. The Headmasters were there, checking in with each of the students, and more than one of his classmates had family members hugging them.

A grin spread over his face when he caught sight of Odele and Adina kissing. So she had healed. Good!

"I'm all right," Wickham said, stroking Rhett's hair.

"Are you sure?" Rhett pulled away and glared at him. "I thought I would have to quit school and get a job to support the family!"

Wickham's brow furrowed. "Did something happen to Mother and Father?"

Rhett scoffed. "No. You were gone."

"But I don't support the family, so why would you—"

"I don't know!" Rhett hugged him again. "I'm just glad that you're back."

Wickham smiled, feeling like a massive weight was lifted off his shoulders. He was back. It was over, and he hoped they had produced a net positive in their wake. "Come on. Let's get inside," he urged. "We have so much to talk about."

<hr />

THE NEXT FEW days were amazing. Kaia had a hot bath every night, finally had the hair products she needed to get the curl back into her hair without being unmanageable, and slept like a baby. Not to mention there was quite the grand feast to celebrate their return, another to celebrate their success in starting peace talks between Lyra and Tidebreaker, and then feasts just for the sake of celebrating.

It was all lovely, but eventually, they had to decide what happened next.

The fourth-year students sat in one classroom, notebooks in hand and everything they had been discussing at the forefront of their minds.

Headmaster Valiant smiled at them as he sat in a chair at the front of the room. Headmaster Twila was to one side of him, while Ealdwulf and West sat to the other side.

Kaia couldn't help but think the four looked highly proud of their students.

"So another quest successfully achieved," Headmaster Twila said, beaming at them. "And so early in the year, too. Now that you all have your kraken's ink, I suppose that means the school year is over. You'll be heading home tomorrow. Goodbye."

Kaia's jaw dropped as the Headmaster got to her feet.

"No, it's not," Herja said, sounding amused and annoyed. "Honestly! That's not even funny."

Headmaster Twila laughed as she settled back down. She winked at Herja. "If you could see your faces, you'd think it was pretty funny."

Headmaster Valiant patted her arm and rolled his eyes. "But in all seriousness, you have all succeeded in your tasks for the semester. The kraken's ink, surviving in an unfamiliar environment, even becoming adept at long-distance mind-to-mind. It puts us in a quandary about what to do with you."

Kaia glanced to her right at Nolen. They had been talking a lot lately about his protective streak and how quickly he turned to a more violent means to defend her.

And they had both decided they knew what they needed to do... but neither liked it.

"Does that mean we can't just stay at the Institute?" Herja asked with a frown.

Headmaster Twila shook her head. "Oh, you can if that's what you want. It's just that the structure for the rest of the year will be a little looser than what you might be used to. If you want to return to your previous camp and have a fresh start, you can. If you want to stay here, you can. You could take the rest of the year off and investigate jobs or spend time with your families."

"The point is, we don't have any particular lessons we need to give you any more," West said.

Ealdwulf nodded. "If you want a regular year, then we can do that. Or we could move the exams early, see how you all do."

Kaia let out a relieved breath. This would make her and Nolen's plan much easier. They would be returning to the seashore. They needed to work together more, to be when they were working together daily.

The problem Nolen had most was that he assumed that because he was the dragon, he was a protector, provider, warrior... all of that.

But the problem was that it automatically made Kaia someone to care for rather than an equal partner in this fated bond, meaning Nolen took on too much. More than Kaia wanted him to. She didn't want to be taken care of and wanted to work together.

So, they needed more time to figure out what that looked like for both. They needed to be when Nolen was forced to step back to let Kaia take care of him sometimes, too.

"And we don't all have to do the same thing, right?" Odele asked.

Kaia shook her head slightly, bringing herself back to the current conversation.

"Right," Headmaster Twila confirmed.

Herja stood up and strode to the front of the classroom. "Thank you, all four of you. Now, I agree we shouldn't all do the same thing," she said as she turned to the group. "However, we should have some structure for the rest of this school year. Perhaps we can have regular returns to the Institute to ensure our self-studying is progressing as it needs to be."

Icarus rested his elbows on his desk. "I second the motion. We all get to decide what we are doing for ourselves, but every six weeks, we return to report on what we are doing and to retake the exams to ensure we aren't slacking."

A few nods answered him.

Kaia cleared her throat as she stood. "Nolen and I will be returning to the sea. Anyone who wishes to come with us is welcome to. However, it's important to note that we will not be working simply on survival. We'll be in contact with Lyra and the krakens regularly."

A few confused glances answered her, but Nolen stood next to her. "Also, we're not getting married. Just to make sure that's clear."

Odele lifted her hand but spoke at the same time. "Does that mean not getting married soon or ever? Because if it's never, I will have to adjust my expectations."

Nolen and Kaia glanced at each other. The two professors and headmasters looked a little startled about this turn of events. But Kaia had told them about Lyra's random insistence that she would throw her and Nolen a wedding, so it wasn't entirely out of pocket.

"Not never," Kaia said with a laugh. "But we have much growing up to do before that. Anyway. Who wants to come with us?"

CHAPTER
TWENTY-NINE

PENELOPE STRETCHED out on her bed, reveling in the faint sound of snowflakes pattering against the window. She had spent the day down in the pond. First, she'd melted the cap of ice off it, then spent the rest of the day practicing her water-dragon existence. She was figuring out how to breathe jets of super-heated water rather than choking on water when she tried to breathe flames.

Have a good day, especially since she didn't have to worry about a mermaid attacking her mate.

Penelope wasn't entirely sure what she would do with herself for the next few months. Since all the students went their own way, she had been thinking about what she could do.

She didn't want to go to the ocean. While part of her wanted to spend more time with Tidebreaker and learn more about the krakens, she felt they would be busy with other things. And she needed time away from Lyra and the mermaids.

Eldavon needed to deal with the situation, and they needed to use a softer hand than Penelope knew she was capable of right now.

Which meant she had plenty more she could do, such as go back to her family in the Fire Watch. Take the entrance tests for the military.

Apply to join a diplomat's mission. Get a job. The possibilities were endless, but also daunting.

A knock came on the door to her room. None of her roommates would knock before entering, so she rolled up to a sitting position. "Come in."

The door opened, and Raven slipped in. Today, they wore a pale blue outfit that went well with their face veil. "You're awake. Good, I was worried you might be sleeping."

Penelope shuffled to one side and patted the bed for Raven to sit. "What's up?"

"I've been talking with the Headmasters," Raven said as they came to lean against the pole of Penelope's four-poster bed. "I've got the kraken's ink, but I have nothing else for my spell book."

Penelope nodded. She felt Raven was leading up to something, though she wasn't sure what that would be. "Do you need one?"

"I think I should have one," Raven replied. "Then I can keep track of everything, you know? My dreams, the correlations I figure out. Even if I don't have spells per se, I could figure out my powers better."

"All right."

"Headmaster Valiant suggested I could spend the rest of the year, until the start of next semester, going on the quests that the witches have already gone on," Raven continued. "The Silent Marsh, the Golden Forest, all that."

Penelope nodded again. She thought she might understand what her mate was getting at, but she worked at stopping herself from jumping to conclusions.

"The thing is, I don't really like the idea of traveling. At least, not with wagon trains and all that," Raven continued. They slid down to sit on the bed next to her. "So, would you go on these quests with me? Flying me from place to place so I don't have to spend too much time in each area?"

A grin burst over Penelope's face. "Would I? I'd love to. We'll have so much fun! And we can have people join us if we want, so we can get to know each other's families better. Last summer was such a whirlwind with all the studying, tests, and whatnot. I don't feel like I got a good chance to get to know your parents."

Raven grasped both of her hands in their own. "I was thinking the same thing."

"Then it's settled! We'll make plans and send out the invitations. It's going to be amazing." Penelope grinned, looking down at where the two of them held hands.

"I'll bring my lap-loom," Raven said happily. "I'll weave our star-threads into a blanket that we can use to keep warm."

"That's perfect."

Despite her happiness, a tiny shred of uncertainty waded through her. While she was determined to make this fated pairing work in whatever way she and Raven felt was best for them, she still wasn't sure what it meant.

And most of all, she wasn't sure if the stars had somehow known that Raven would be a gorgon and so had planned to pair them together from the start...

Or if they had been matched simply because they were both there and neither had any other mates.

She shook off the thought. The stars didn't make mistakes like that. She was bonded to Raven for a reason. And they were going to make a perfect pairing.

❦

NOLEN RUBBED Kaia's feet as they sat in the common area of the dorm room. The two of them had been very busy today, running around like chickens as they made sure all their things were packed and ready to head back to the sea. They'd be heading out tomorrow.

Now, Kaia's feet were aching, and she lay with her feet in Nolen's lap. He massaged the aches away while staring broodingly into the fire.

Lena and Victor talked in a low voice at the table while Odele and Adina curled up on the floor next to the fireplace, looking like a couple of cats. Odele's head rested on Adina's stomach, and Adina played with Odele's hair with her eyes closed.

"You look like you're having doubts," Kaia noted, propping her head beneath her arm.

Nolen looked up. "Er... yeah. Yeah, I'm having doubts."

"Do you want to talk about it?"

Nolen switched to her second foot, making her first one feel a little cool. "Welllllll... I don't know. I don't want to change my mind. I feel like this is the best option for us as mates and individually. I just. I hope it is the best option. And that we're not, you know, taking on more than we should."

Kaia nodded her understanding. She had wrestled with it herself. There was no guarantee that she would be helpful in the talks between mermaids and krakens. She was still furious with Lyra for taking advantage of her and herself for letting it go on for so long.

"I know that it's difficult, but I think it's going to work out just fine," she said, pulling her foot away. She sat up and took hold of Nolen's hands. "You said you wanted to work with the sea after we graduated. I didn't know what I wanted to do, but now I see that there is something I can do."

"I know. I just feel like maybe we're expecting too much of ourselves. Or maybe just that it feels like we're already working as diplomats with none of the training," he said with a shrug.

Kaia nodded at that. She felt the same way. At least she had family members who were ambassadors, and she had heard plenty about it. She had integrated with all levels of the government. Nolen hadn't. Given that he was an introvert to boot, it was no wonder why the circumstances they'd found themselves put him on edge.

"We're not going to live in Lyra's city," she reminded herself and him. "We're going to be part of the domestic labor force in the camp Eldavon is establishing to facilitate peace talks between Lyra, the krakens, and the other cities."

"Domestic labor force," Nolen repeated. He cracked a grin at her. "I like the sound of that."

Kaia squeezed his hand. "I know it's too much to ask to say that we won't have to deal with Lyra or the mermaids at all. But there will be others to take care of the big stuff. It won't be a diplomatic mission like when we visited Odentia last year."

"I know."

Kaia squeezed his hand again. "And maybe once it's summer, we can break away again. We'll find a nice patch of forest to homestead on with Odele and Adina. Or we could go back to the Silent Marsh. Anything you want."

Nolen cracked a grin at her as he leaned forward. His lips pressed to her forehead, and Kaia sighed in delight. She loved it so much when he kissed her forehead.

Nolen nodded towards the letter Kaia had received from Odentia's queen, asking her to come to Odentia again. She had received it just that morning. Kaia was surprised; she hadn't thought she had made that big of an impression on the queen, not when so many other people were with them.

"What does it say?" he asked.

"It's an invitation to spend a few weeks in her court," Kaia said.

Nolen frowned. "If you want to do that instead—"

"I don't." She sighed and leaned back on the couch. "Tomorrow, I plan to write a letter back, thanking her but explaining how it's impossible now. There's too much history with Odentia."

Nolen cracked a smile. "And there isn't with Lyra?"

"Domestic labor, remember? We wouldn't get that with Odentia."

"I suppose." Nolen stretched his arms over her head and stifled a yawn. "It seems like we have quite the responsibility here at home, anyway."

Kaia gazed into the fire, watching the flames flicker this way and that. She felt a little like that flame, uncertain where to go next, unsure where she stood. She wanted to plant her feet firmly on the ground, but where was she needed the most?

Right now, her mate needed her the most. She needed to work on her relationship with Nolen. They needed to trust each other more deeply, which meant that Odentia's young queen would just have to wait.

"This is okay with you, right?" she asked in worry, lifting her face back to Nolen's.

"What is?"

"Going to the sea and joining with this mission, instead of staying here or going back to your home. I know you said you're okay with it, but you're not just saying that right?" she searched his expression. "You're not just going along with the plans I made?"

"Those are plans *we* made, Kaia," he assured her.

Her shoulders relaxed, and she smiled at him. "Good."

"I'm looking forward to a lot of things we'll be doing at the seashore," he continued. "Learning more about what the coastal watch does will be good because you're right. One day, I want to work on the sea."

He grinned at her, and Kaia smiled back. This felt like an adventure —and she couldn't wait to get started.

CHAPTER

THIRTY

A MONTH after the students returned to the Institute, it was time for winter break. Herja was surprised at how much time had passed while they were in the mermaid city. It had felt like so much longer and so much shorter.

It was winter break. And Herja, Wickham, Row, and Row's mate were at the orphanage where Herja grew up.

Herja blinked rapidly as she sat at Mr. Bryce's desk. Several of the other caregivers were here as witnesses as Row and their mate filled out the paperwork. She hadn't expected to feel this emotional. She'd expected to continue to wonder if it was worth it to go through all the effort of being adopted.

Mr. Bryce gave her a beaming, watery smile as he handed her a paper as well. "All right. So you just have to sign here, stating that this is what you want."

Herja took the pen from him and stared down at the adoption papers. For years she'd wanted to be adopted, and now it seemed almost too easy to see it happen finally. Row and their mate beamed at her, and she grinned back, warmth flooding her chest.

She signed the papers... and for the first time since she was a little girl, she was once again someone's daughter.

Her lip trembled with the crash of emotions that came down on her, and Wickham squeezed her free hand.

"Sorry, I don't know why I'm being such a baby," Herja mumbled, wiping away the tears that streamed down her cheeks.

Row put their arm around her and hugged her tight. They said nothing, but they didn't need to. She was adopted. She had a family.

"I can't tell you how happy I am for you, Herja," Mr. Bryce said, wiping at a few tears of his own. "I always knew one day you'd find your family."

"Thanks," Herja whispered.

Mr. Bryce cleared his throat and collected the paperwork again, making sure everything was signed and witnessed according to the regulations. "So, what are your plans now? I heard that this year's students weren't having a normal school year at the Institute."

Herja smiled, grateful for the change of subject. Not that she wasn't grateful to be adopted—she certainly was. It was just that she didn't want to keep crying, even if they were happy tears.

She straightened slightly as she cleared the lump of emotion from her throat. "I'm staying at the Institute for the next semester. I will act as a helper in the classes taught to the younger students, so I can better understand what it's like to interact with kids."

Mr. Bryce looked surprised. "Oh? When did this happen?"

"Over the summer. Wickham and I nearly broke up because he wants kids someday, and I'm not sure. But I did decide I want to be in education, and I just need to interact more with younger people before deciding which area to pursue."

Row gave her a pointed look. "But you also decided that you would both wait for the kid's question, right?"

"Right." Herja's brow furrowed. She had told Row about this already —but no, this was for Mr. Bryce's benefit. She laughed as she turned to him and his stunned expression. "That's right. When I said Wickham wants kids, I mean some day after he's graduated from medical school."

Mr. Bryce let out a relieved-sounding sigh.

Herja rested her hands on the desk, smiling at the paperwork now. It felt like it had taken her a long time to get here, but it was well worth it. She was adopted now. She had her mate and a plan for moving forward in her future.

She sighed happily as she beamed at all the people around her. "I never would have gotten to where I am without all of you. Thank you so much. You all helped me in ways I can't—" She got choked up and cleared her throat. "I can't express."

"You're not the only one who has gotten help," Wickham told her. He kissed her cheek as they stood. "I love you. So much."

"I love you, too." Herja squeezed his hand and then reached for Rows. "Come on. I want to show you my favorite old haunts. We'll start with the library. The librarian, Libby, was the one who gave me my bookbag."

Wickham nodded as they headed out; they'd stop by again later to get copies of the adoption paperwork.

"You know what?" Herja mused as they stepped into the bright winter's day. "This was the first year we didn't use it as a vital survival tool."

"Huh." Wickham shrugged. "I guess we didn't. I hope it didn't get jealous."

Herja laughed. Today was, she thought, the best day of her life.

⁂

WICKHAM GRINNED as Rhett ran on ahead toward their house. After Herja's adoption, they had spent a few days in her hometown, and now Herja was back at the Institute while Wickham brought Rhett home. She'd come to celebrate the Winter's Feast later in the year.

Rhett opened the door and bolted in, neglecting to close it again. "I'm baaaaack!" he called.

Laughing, Wickham hurried after him and closed the door. An explosion of excitement greeted him as Rhett and Donnelly talked over each other, both trying to tell the other everything that had happened to them over the semester. Tara jumped around here and there, begging for attention.

Mother skirted around the younger kids and hugged Wickham. She kissed his temple. "I'm glad you're home."

"Me, too," he murmured. "I'll tell you everything that happened with the mermaids once they're all in bed."

He gestured vaguely to his younger siblings, then embraced Father. Father ruffled his hair and patted his back. "The hero has returned."

"Yeah," Tara shouted. "Wick the hero!"

Wickham laughed. "Wick the hero, huh? Well, that sounds pretty nice. And what about you? Are you Tara the Math Whiz?"

Tara grinned. "I am. I know alllll the pluses by myself!"

For the next few hours, it was loveable chaos. Rhett demonstrated everything he had learned in his first year at the Institute while Donnelly kept running to his room to bring back the trinkets he had made throughout the semester.

"Next semester, I'm going into advanced woodworking," Donnelly said enthusiastically. He gave Rhett a small shield carved with the image of a stylized dragon's head. "My teachers say I have a lot of talent. I think I might be a carpenter or a wagon captain when I grow up."

Tara climbed into Wickham's lap with a piece of paper. "See? One plus one is two. One plus two is three...."

Wickham let the noise wash over him. There once was a time he'd ended up in an anxiety attack whenever he thought about his family without him. Now, as he looked back, he didn't know why he was so determined that they couldn't get on without him.

They were all strong, intelligent, and hardworking. They were all thriving, and he couldn't be happier for all of them. Seeing how well they were getting on didn't make him feel unneeded. It just emphasized how much he had to give to others.

Knowing how much they were thriving eased so much of the burden off his shoulders.

"Is anyone going to ask Wickham what he will do next?" Mother asked in a slightly chiding tone after some time.

The twins and Tara had settled down but were still discussing

Donnelly's prospects. Wickham opened his mouth to protest—they were exemplary in their topic; he didn't need any special attention.

Donnelly, however, turned very serious as he faced his older brother. "I'm sorry. I forgot to ask. I guess I'm just used to you always having everything already in order."

"It's fine, Don. Well, since things happened a little weird for me this last semester, I'm not going back to the Institute until next year," he explained. He had been busy these last few weeks arranging everything.

"You're not?" Rhett asked, his expression faltering. "But we're supposed to be there together."

Wickham laughed and ruffled Rhett's hair affectionately. "I know. Herja will still be there, though. The thing is, I'm going to start medical school. I want to get a good start on it and help people better than I have the skills for."

Rhett folded his arms and sighed. "Well, I guess that's reasonable enough."

He looked so much like a grumpy old man that Wickham had to laugh again. "You're going to have an outstanding semester. Much better than if your big brother was there to be worried about you all the time."

"I guess."

"But it also means that I'm going to be spending a lot of time over the winter break studying," Wickham told them. "I won't have a lot of time to play. But I promise to make time for you all."

Tara bounced on her knees. "I'll help you study. I'm smart at learning things."

"Me, too," Donnelly agreed.

"We all will," Father said.

Wickham looked around at his family, grinning. His siblings were growing up, and everyone was thriving. He'd been through yet another situation that he thought was too big for him, but with the help of his friends, he pulled through.

He was going to be okay. They all were. And he couldn't wait until next year when he'd meet up with all his friends again and face their next adventure together.

The End

If you enjoyed this book, please consider leaving a review on
Goodreads, Bookbub or your favorite retailer.
Reviews help me reach new readers.

Read *The Quest for the Kraken's Ink*, the fourth book in the *Defenders of the Realm* series!

OR

Read *A Summer of Destiny*, the third Fantasy Romance Novella in the *Defenders of the Realm* series!

OR

Have you read the prequel?
A Journey to Power

Join my Newsletter for writing updates, sales and giveaways!
www.mhlebeault.com